BENEATH THE SALTON SEA

MICHAEL PAUL GONZALEZ

PMMP

Perpetual Motion Machine Publishing
Cibolo, Texas

Beneath the Salton Sea
Copyright © 2021 Michael Paul Gonzalez

ISBN: 978-1-943720-65-1

www.PerpetualPublishing.com

Cover Picture by Aleks Bieńkowska

ADVANCE PRAISE FOR
BENEATH THE SALTON SEA

you are not lost
you are here
and you are loved
start again

I.
HOW THE LIGHT GETS IN

2008-pause-2012

YOU WILL HEAR *her voice when you try to sleep.*
This was written in bright orange paint marker in desperate, trembling letters on the wall of a religious alcove. It stood out among the small paintings of saints and messages of hope that adorned Salvation Mountain. When we first saw it, we thought it was desecration, some drug-addled kid trying to paint their demons on the wall. It was a warning, as close to a message from God as we would get. We just didn't have eyes to see it yet.

Eight miles away from the Salton Sea, a quick stop to film some B-roll and see the sights out in the middle of the vast nothing. Salvation Mountain was a singular work of insanity or religious devotion, depending on your perspective. Thousands of gallons of paint, hay, glue, and trash sculpted in the desert as a last refuge. Look up some photos. Nothing I say could do it justice, our little off-ramp to hell.

A little way up the road was Slab City, an enclave of people who'd reclaimed an abandoned artillery range in the desert, parked their motor homes, and started a strange off-the-grid community. Sharon and I were there

1

to interview the residents and document their lives for a fluff piece on the late news back in L.A. The state government was getting ready to impose some water restrictions and rezoning ordinances, and the locals were ready to fight. It was exactly as exciting as it sounds. Still, we'd needed an excuse to get away from the city and spend more time together. Sharon loved camping. I am not a fan of the outdoors, but I loved her more than I hated dirt, so what was a girl to do?

I don't know if the locals were always open and friendly, but they were nice enough to us. We set up our camera by an old spindly tree decorated with countless shoes strung by their laces. Dozens of locals were hanging around that day, every one of them demanding to say their piece on camera, hopeful we'd get the message out to anyone who might sympathize with their quest for freedom and lend support. They wanted us to understand what brought them to the desert and what stopped them from going back to civilization.

That's all I want. Why I'm writing this. I want you to understand what brought us out to the desert and what we left there.

After we wrapped, we got to talking to a couple of the locals and decided to camp at Slab City for the night. They took us everywhere, insistent we document the lives they'd created so the world wouldn't think they were just a bunch of freeloading hippies in the desert. There was an open air installation called East Jesus that had nothing to do with religion and everything to do with turning garbage into beautiful art. Houses, bike repair shops, craftsmen, artisans plying their trade. When the sun started going down, they took us to The Range, a stage and open air restaurant where the locals gathered every Saturday for food, music, and stories.

Somewhere around our fourth beer or fifth joint, one of them asked if we'd heard of the crack in the sky over the

Salton Sea. She was all leathery skin and grey dreadlocks, told us about how she'd moved to the desert when her husband was serving with the Marines during the birth of the Cold War. She said there were things he was privy to that got him killed. He would tell her about these experiments they ran out in the restricted area, way back in Patton's day. Something worse-than-nuclear that did more than split atoms. One of those world-enders that the military likes to call peacekeepers. She said he knew too much about it and that's why they killed him.

Sharon whispered to me that he probably ran off with one of the younger, smoother hippie chicks. I started to pull out the camera, then felt a warm hand rest softly but firmly on my forearm.

"Just let her alone." An old man from the next table over squeezed my arm, two gentle pulses. He murmured in my ear, "She'll stop talking soon enough. You're here to help us, right? You put Doreen on camera and it'll scuttle the whole thing. I used to do what you did, way back in the day. I get it. But can you just take the rest of the night off and enjoy the music? We've been nothing but nice to you."

Sharon pursed her lips and nodded at me, hoisting her beer bottle. "Dee's a workaholic. It's one of the things we fight about at home."

I slid the camera back into my bag and picked up my beer bottle. "All work and no play."

"No such thing out here." The old guy smiled at me. "And thank you kindly."

It was one of those *thank yous* that was tinged with a healthy dose of *fuck you*. I didn't want to wear out our welcome. This was the closest thing to a date night that Shar and I had had in a long time.

Doreen smiled at us through the whole exchange. "Are you two married?"

"We've been talking about it."

"For a long time," Sharon said. "A really long time."

"It's legal now, right?"

"Just barely."

"What are you waiting for?"

"What *are* we waiting for, Dee?"

"What was your marriage like?" I asked Doreen.

She jumped right back into her conspiracy story, said the night before he disappeared, her husband told her to watch the sky at noon because something was going to happen that would change the world. She took their car up to the top of a ridge with a pair of his field glasses and watched where he told her to watch. There was no explosion, she said. Just a weird ripple in the air that she kept calling the crack in the sky. He didn't make it home from work that day. Nobody came to inform her that he'd deserted or died. Everyone they'd known on base got transferred. Nobody would talk to her. They just erased him. Both of them, really. No benefits for her. No memories. She said they stole all of his photos while she slept, his clothes too. Like she'd never been married.

"That was the worst part. All of those years, everything we built. All of the little things, you know? His face? His smell. His . . . you know, everything." She seemed lost in the moment. "I had friends, people I used to write to every week. They'd get suspicious if I stopped, you know? I think that's why they didn't come after me, too. Ray's only friends were in the service, and they were loyal to the Corps. If they had anything to tell me about what happened to him, they didn't say boo."

The old guy wandered back to our table and touched Doreen's shoulder. "It's getting late, Doreen. I don't want you wandering in the middle of the night. Let me get you home."

She reluctantly stood up. "If you have radios, you can go out there and hear it. Probably film it too. Forget this water rights stuff. There's bigger things the people need to know about. Go to Bombay Beach where the ground is burned."

"All right, Doreen." He turned her by the shoulder and glanced at us as he walked away.

"Such interesting people." Sharon buzzed her lips against my neck.

The music and festivities were still going, and the booze had worked its way nicely into my blood. Sharon asked me to dance, and we did. We forgot about Doreen and got lost in a haze of smoke and hooch and good music. When we went back to our little pup tent at the end of the night, I asked Sharon what she thought of the story.

"Probably a crack in her brain from too much acid."

"Yeah, but we should check it out, right? We're headed that way anyway to get back home. Might make an interesting pitch for another story."

She kissed me on the lips. "I'm really high." I kissed her back and we found our way out of our clothes and into our sleeping bag.

The next morning, I woke up cold. The old woman sat cross-legged outside our tent, staring at us.

"You believed me, right?" Doreen asked.

"Sure." I wiped sleep from my eyes and nudged Sharon awake.

She giggled and turned away from the tent opening. "Nothing I haven't seen before. But the crack in the sky, you ladies can see it. Turn your head to the ground and use your peripheral vision. If you're near the north end of the sea, you see it out of the corner of your eye. It never stopped. It's still there, letting things in. He died for it. They took my Raymond because he knew too much. You drive by Bombay Beach and you'll see the burn in the ground from where the bomb went off. Around midnight, you turn your radio on AM to the end of the dial. The voices will come. That's your story right there. People need to know."

Her eyes were shiny and wet, somewhere far away. She wasn't looking at us, just staring through the tent into some past catastrophe.

"We need to get dressed and ready for the day, Doreen."

"Okay," she said. Then, "Oh! Oh my, where are my manners? You ladies get dressed. I'll make you a sack lunch to take with you."

"That sounds nice, Doreen, thank you."

She tottered to her feet and crunched away through the gravel.

"Why would you bother that sweet lady to make lunch for us?" Sharon whispered.

"She left, didn't she?"

Sharon took my hand and caressed my cheek.

"This was nice, Shar. I'm . . . I really hate camping, you know. But this was nice." I smiled at her and spun around, leaning into her and snapping a picture of the two of us with my little Canon point and shoot. We looked terrible. No makeup, bedhead, bleary-eyed. But she had that smile that I loved so much, that half-grin, those fretting eyebrows, tongue half-out. That was the last good picture of us. The last good moment, really.

We loaded the car to head out, shook a few hands, took contact info, promised we'd do what we could to get their story to the masses. We had just started to roll out on the main road when Sharon tapped my arm. "There's our crazy friend."

Doreen, waving a sack wildly above her head, doing that weird chicken walk some older people do when they need to move quickly. Her face was more wrinkle than skin, her smile more open space than tooth. I rolled down my window and she thrust the sack through into my lap.

"Hi, Doreen."

"There's notes in there that you'll need. Didn't have much for food, so I hope you like peanut butter and apple sandwiches. Couple bottles of water. And some masks. You'll thank me later for that. You need those when you're poking around in the rundown houses."

"You think we'd want to?"

"Nobody thinks they do until they see them."

"Okay, Doreen. Thank you for all of this. We've gotta hit the road."

"To Bombay Beach?"

"We'll . . . yeah, we've got a couple of stops on our way out. We'll hit up Bombay Beach. Promise. We might see you again if things pan out, okay?"

"Oh, I hope so. I hope so. As soon as the sun starts going down, they'll start singing to you. Believe me. Just listen. Open ears, open minds."

I gave her a thumbs up. Don't know why, I never do that. We drove off. Sharon was quiet, breathing heavy through her nose. She usually did that when she felt carsick. That also meant she would be grumpy all day.

"You have fun last night?" I squeezed her thigh.

"Yes I did. Maybe too much. My stomach is feeling a little off. Did you drink any of that bottle they were passing around?"

"Probably?" I laughed. "I wasn't really saying no to anything. When in Rome . . . "

We were five miles outside of Slab City, riding smooth and quiet, when she picked up the bag Doreen gave us. "Why don't you ever tell people we're married?"

"I do."

"I mean, sort of. Inside our protective L.A. bubble, maybe. Even then your default answer is always to make jokes." She kept rolling and unrolling the top of the bag.

"I'm . . . I don't know. Protective."

"You don't have to be. It's 2008. I'd like to be us. Everywhere. We travel a lot for work. It's the best and worst part of the job, because I get to be with you and we have to be separate because of . . . what? Can you at least hold my hand?"

"Do we have to get into this now? This was a good weekend."

"Yes! A good weekend. And it's been a good couple of married months. I think. After a good couple of regular years. Sometimes I . . . Doreen, her marriage was real, right? You believe her? And she says it's all gone now. No record of it. I don't know what you're scared of, but she has the weight of the . . . the fucking Deep State coming after her marriage, and she still talks about it . . . "

"*Sharon* . . . "

"Oh God, the sing-song. Okay. Okay, never mind."

"There is *plenty* of record of our marriage. Pictures, and . . . trips . . . and do we have to do this now?"

"I guess not." She opened the bag and started poking around. The sandwiches Doreen made were remarkably clean-cut, perfect squares with the crusts cut off, thin slices of apple and peanut butter in between slightly crusty white bread. There were two more apples inside the bag, and another smaller brown bag. That one held two paper N95 masks nested inside of each other and a faded picture of a man in military uniform.

It was a formal portrait, his jacket starched, hat perfectly poised on a head that was faded and scratched from years of riding in someone's pocketbook. I couldn't make out his face, but behind the creases and small flakes in the paper, pareidolia created an unsettling skeletal grimace in its place. "That her husband? I thought she said they erased every trace of him."

"She also said there's a crack in the sky, Dee. The back of the photo says . . . something. I can't make it out. A love note, I guess. It's got her name at the top and some scribbling underneath."

"Sweet."

"You want to check it out, don't you?"

"You're in a hurry to get back to L.A. and hand over the bumpkin interview spectacular?" I poked her stomach. "We're off today and tomorrow, might as well take advantage, right?"

"Yeah, take advantage of a free day back home. Shower three times to get all of this dust off. Catch a movie, go to dinner . . ."

"Come on, Sharon. I've heard about Bombay Beach. I think it'll be pretty cool."

"You've heard about all that shit she said?"

"Not the crack stuff, just . . . it's like this tiny little town that got wiped out in a flood years ago. The houses are falling down, there's like . . . boats and pianos and cars and stuff sticking out of the mud. All sorts of cool graffiti and houses falling down, and . . . come on! You like street art, right? I've heard it's a haven for taggers."

"Taggers," she scoffed. "Fine. A quick stop."

You will hear their voices when you try to sleep etched in bright orange paint marker on the inside of an exposed doorframe on a burned-out trailer home.

"So this one says 'their' voices. Remember the thing we saw at Salvation Mountain? That one said 'her' voice. Looks like the same handwriting to me." Sharon snapped a picture with her phone.

It had become a game. Maybe we were killing time. Maybe we were subtly trying to convince each other that there was something to Doreen's story. It was pretty clear that we'd end up at the North Shore before the end of the day to turn our radios on and hear what we could hear.

We poked around a few abandoned houses and then drove the car to the water's edge. A big dirt flood wall separated the town and the sea with a ramp going up so cars could park. If the town was an apocalyptic wasteland, what lay over the ridge was the end of all creation. The shoreline was dotted with rusted cars, the skeletons of trailers and beach houses, and every kind of trash imaginable.

The wind carried the stench of the Salton Sea away

from us, and it was pleasant enough that we sat on the hood scarfing down Doreen's sandwiches, which were surprisingly delicious. The water tasted a little off. Probably well water or maybe it had been sitting on a shelf somewhere for way too long.

I had this notion that I should say something to Sharon. I wondered if she felt the same. We both kind of stopped chewing at the same time and looked at each other, then smiled. And I guess I could read that as comfort, or ease. But I wonder if she felt what I did. I wonder if there was something she wished I would say, or if she knew what I wished she would say. I didn't know what I wanted to hear. I took the last bit of crust and tossed it toward the sea.

"For the birds," I muttered. I flicked a finger toward the ground just past where the bread landed, standing up slowly.

On the west end of the beach, if you could call it that, there really was a dark line in the ground, about five feet wide, black as coal. Was it there before we started eating?

It faded about ten feet from the shore, a small patch of scorched earth half-buried in silt and powdered fish bones. There was a curve to it. I imagine if you traced that arc it would be an inverted-U shape cutting out of water that encircled most of the small rotting enclaves remaining near the northern half of the Salton Sea.

"Once you cross black, you don't cross back," Sharon joked as we walked across the expanse of charred earth. She got halfway across when she turned a quick 180 and walked away, planting her feet in the untarnished dirt. She folded her arms across her stomach, keeping her back turned on the line.

"Did you feel that? It's cold, it's . . . weird. That's weird."

"Just the breeze, girl. Don't go crazy on me now." I'd felt it too, a push of air like cold water surging around me.

To give voice to that would have pushed me over the edge. I probably would have gotten in the car and headed home to L.A. to drink away the rest of our day off.

I crossed the small expanse and looked back. That was the first time I noticed the stillness, standing there on the opposite side of the line from her. No birds. No breeze. No rustling of leaves, although the few nearby trees swayed and I felt the wind on my face. I extended my hand to Sharon. "Come hug me. Here, in public. In front of everyone!" I spun a wide circle, indicating the vast emptiness around us.

She turned to me, that crooked smile of hers that always tugged at my heart, and I wanted nothing more than to march across that line and take her in my arms.

"We're on an adventure," I said. "To boldly go." My feet felt anchored, rooted into the hardpan. I shuddered, then lifted first one foot, then the other. Stepped back into the black, walked to her, wrapped my arms around her. "See? Don't let the old wives' tales fool you. We're done here anyway. We'll go check out the northern shore, put the radio on, listen to all of the nothing that comes through, call it a ruined night and head home. What do you say?"

She took a deep breath and kept her eyes down, the toe of her boot digging a line on the rough gravel in front of the charred black. "You're so romantic." She sighed, looking up at me. "Did you just call me your old wife?"

"I'll be *your* old wife. One of these days."

She smiled and took my hand. She brought it to her mouth, then kissed it, drawing back suddenly. "You feel . . . bloodless."

"Just a little cold. You don't have to be mean about it!"

"I'm . . . I don't even know why that word came to me." She briskly rubbed my hand, making a show of breathing her hot breath on it.

We walked together across the line and explored Bombay Beach. The houses all looked like they shared

11

some disease, like they'd gotten diarrhea and unleashed their bowels. Trash everywhere. But inside, stepping over the shattered furniture, the broken bricks and skeletal two-by-fours, we found art that was insanely beautiful. Giant political paste-ups, airbrushed pinup girls, multicolored stencils and cryptic messages. I snapped a few pictures, wondering who I'd show this to. The farther we put the black line in the sand behind us, the cooler it got. The weather hadn't changed. The sky was just as mercilessly cloudless, the sun still bright enough to peel paint off the decaying trailers, but it was unmistakably a few degrees cooler here than it had been back at the car.

The only noise was the crunch of our boots on broken masonry and glass. Our footsteps weren't loud exactly, but intense. Every noise came sharp, harsh. The swish of an arm as it swept across the body. Inner thighs whipping past each other. The aglet of a shoelace ticking against the side of a shoe. A tiny pebble skittering underfoot. All of it reported with the clarity of a gunshot on a still morning. If we stopped moving, everything grew painfully silent beyond the rasp of our breath.

I think we both noticed it, but neither of us said anything.

I thought about a trip we'd taken before to shoot a doc at Birkenau in Poland, trying to work with an Electronic Voice Phenomena "expert." Row after row of empty buildings. The only thing more unsettling than the feeling of being watched was the knowledge that nobody was there to see us. Bombay Beach felt the same. We walked, keeping our eyes low until we got back to the car.

Finally, Sharon whispered, "You hear that?"

"What?"

"Exactly."

"This is weird, right?"

"Yeah."

"But we have to go check out the North Shore, right? I mean . . . we *have* to, now. Right?"

"It looks like other people have tried." She pointed to another paint marker tag on a doorframe that said *The voices come when the stars fall.*

We took a few more pictures, prodded at some of the broken glass, the boards, the pieces of appliances and furniture. I got some wide shots on video, mindful of the need to conserve batteries. If nothing else, I could smack together five minutes of footage that would convince the network higher-ups to send us back out here for a story.

"You think the Yacht Club will be as fancy as this place?"

Sharon smiled a little, but her cheek dipped in. She was biting it, a tell I'd learned to spot that meant she was nervous. I started the car and we rolled out.

Everything had a strange, muted quality. Tires crunching on gravel, the breeze coming through the cracked windows, the engine pitching up and down as it shifted through gears.

Sharon turned the radio over to AM and scanned through the high and low ends of the frequencies. The static would grow quieter as she reached the extreme ends until they hit silence. She eventually gave up and kept her arms folded, eyes out the window. I kept checking the temperature on the dash. We'd been sweating in ninety-five-degree heat back at Slab City. We were only a few miles down the road and the thermometer read seventy-two degrees.

We drove in silence to the northern point of the sea, the fabled North Shore Yacht Club. It had died an undignified death decades ago, its corpse slowly rotting by the water. The locals harbored no illusions about a return to the grandeur of the Desert Riviera era, but they were still proud enough to eliminate as many eyesores as possible. They wanted to make an honest go of it, determined to hold on to their dignity. There were plans to refurbish this mess into a visitor's center. Seemed like everything was on hold for the immediate . . . forever.

We pulled into the dirt lot. The entire building was boarded up. Intricate murals battled against sloppy signatures and meth-laced paint bombs. Even the broken pylons that jutted from the water a few feet from the shoreline were tattooed in spray-paint.

"Sixty-four degrees," I muttered as I got out of the car. The sun was still high. This wasn't the season for cold snaps. Faded yellow plastic caution tape floated like party streamers on a silent breeze by the front door. We walked from the parking lot to the edge of the building, standing near the remains of a cinderblock bait house. I snapped a wide angle shot.

LISTEN.

The word was spray-painted over and over again in a repeating line stretching the length of the building. Someone had drawn crude stars spilling out of one of the upstairs windows.

Sharon moved beside me, shouldering her backpack. "You ready to finish this uneventful evening?"

"You planning on a hike?"

"I'm not going into that creepy fucking place without every light source we have. We have two radios and three recorders."

"You believe her? And what do you mean going in?"

"I want to see what's in there. Might as well kill some time before the show starts, right? We're here to look for the crack in the sky, see something exciting, whatever it is you want to do to avoid . . . Anyway, I'd rather go inside while we still have some daylight."

"We don't have to do this, you know. I just thought it would be fun."

"It's fun! We're having fun. This is fun. Let's have fun."

I pulled my gear bag out of the trunk, testing my flashlight and checking batteries on my recorders. I don't know how this had turned into a semi-silent argument, but here we were. Checking devices, looking at each other, looking at the building, at the parking lot, the sky. Both of us waiting for the other to take the first step. I wasn't going to press the issue. I had things I could have complained about too. Three of them racing up from my lungs and through my mouth, but what came out was, "I have an idea!" I said it so suddenly that it startled Sharon. "We set up a recording station out here. Let it run for a few hours and see if it picks anything up while we're exploring."

"Are we ghost hunters now?"

"Every good reporter is a ghost hunter."

"Probably just burnouts squatting in there."

"We take off at the first sign of occupancy, deal?" I gave her a thumbs up.

"You don't have to tell me twice."

We set up our outdoor audio listening station. I aimed the camera at the front door, set the video for the lowest quality that would still give acceptable quality to maximize recording time. I taped an mp3 recorder to the front leg and hit record.

"This should give us a few hours. I mean. Not that we need it, we'll be back long before that."

"You still have that thing?"

"First one I bought and she's never failed. I'm loyal." I kissed two fingers and tapped the fading blue plastic on the front of the mp3 player. The black and white LCD screen was cracked, making the display splotchy in places, but it was always there for me.

The sun was getting lower. When I moved my head quickly, I thought I saw a ripple in the sky over the sea southeast of the building. It wasn't quite a crack, more like a fold, a darkening of color, and it was only there when I wasn't really trying to find it.

"You see it?"

Sharon shrugged. "The sea?"

"Nah, the uh . . . never mind. You ready to go inside?"

"You got a knife on you?"

"What are you planning, Katniss?"

"Don't make fun. We don't know who's in there, but if anyone is, we need to be ready. I've got one. Pepper spray too."

"Fine. You hear me scream, then come running with your pig-sticker. It's gonna be hard enough to breathe in there from all the rotten . . . rot. Maybe keep the safety on the pepper spray."

Unease settled around my shoulders like a cold, wet blanket. I suddenly wanted this to be done. But I couldn't stop. Something here was worth hanging around.

I walked back toward the Yacht Club, hoping my strut looked more like confidence and not nervous energy. The main doors had been blown out long ago, replaced with crude plywood to keep the elements out. I peeked through the uneven gap between the doors. It was dark inside, small pools of light thrown here and there through holes in the roof and walls. The place had been locked up, but the center of the doorline, where you'd expect to find handles, looked like an angry animal had torn through with sharp teeth. The remains lay on the dirt, a padlocked loop of rusted chain like an intestine, the two metal braces that had been screwed into the plywood still attached. I swept it aside with my foot and pulled one door open.

Someone had spray-painted NO CALLS AFTER SUNDOWN in four-foot-high orange letters on the wall in the hallway. We stood beneath the shattered remains of a light fixture designed to look like a boat was sailing above us. The lobby was as amazing to see as it was wretched to smell. Salty air, bird shit, human waste, rotting wood, dead fish brought in by the seagulls. All of it piled beneath beautiful, airbrushed murals, illegible phrases and giant paste-ups. There were rusted lawn chairs, eviscerated loveseats, desks that looked like palsied old men leaning back against the wall. Sharon pulled out the paper masks Doreen had given us.

"Guess she gave these to us for a reason. Put it on. Keep it on. We're gonna be kicking up a lot of nasty shit moving through here. Sundown in about an hour if you—" It was like someone turned the volume down on her voice. She was still talking, then waiting for an answer. She tilted her head, gesticulating.

"What's that?"

"Two hours." She tapped her wrist. I only knew she was talking because of the way the paper mask moved on her face.

I held up a finger and quietly asked, "Can you hear me?"

She nodded.

"Tell me you can hear me."

Her mask moved and I heard nothing.

"Louder."

"Stop fucking around, Dee!"

This time I heard her just fine.

There was a torn sheet of notebook paper on one of the chairs in a corner, held down by a chunk of cinder block. Tiny, intense handwriting crammed into the corner of the page, the rest of it blank, strange designs etched into the paper with a dead pen.

First the tide will rise. After sundown. The breeze. Then the birds. Isn't the season for insects, but maybe you'll hear a few. Then you'll grow tired. Then I'll come to you.

"What do you think that means?" I gestured for Sharon to come look at it.

"Nothing. It's . . . wait . . . " She cocked her head, then fumbled in her pocket and pulled out the photo Doreen had given us, flipping it over and holding it side-by-side with the paper. "Okay, that's weird."

"Same handwriting?"

"I mean . . . I'm not an expert, but . . . "

"What do you think she . . . Doreen? Doreen!" I called her name out a few times, convinced she'd come around the corner smiling at us.

"I don't think she's here, Dee. Pretty sure we're alone."

"Let's look around and get some video and get the fuck out. It's too cold in here."

Sharon headed for a staircase at the far end of a long hallway lit by dusty shafts of dying light. I called out to her to stop but she just kept moving. She turned when she got to the foot of the stairs and stared at me. I looked back at her. Finally her head started to bob and she stuck her arms out as if to ask me what the hell I was waiting for. I hustled down the hallway to the staircase.

"You didn't hear me?"

I shook my head. "I was asking you to hold up."

"I didn't hear you." She clapped her hands together twice. It sounded like she had thick woolen gloves on. "Weird. Turn your radio on. Might as well go full crazy if we're going, right?"

"You sound like you have a pillow over your face."

We looked at each other, sharing what I assumed was an uneasy smile beneath our masks. It was actually happening. It's one thing to read about going to the moon, an entirely different thing to take that first step into the void.

We hustled up the stairs, mindful of the way the wood creaked and popped as we passed over it. The landing branched off into two long hallways. One of them was dark and littered with broken furniture and debris. We chose the one lit by a series of holes in the roof and light streaming in from rooms on the side. Neon-colored streaks of paint marker, bright oranges, pinks, whites, and silver ran the length of the walls and tapered down as they reached a doorway at the far end of the hall. That door was surrounded by crudely drawn stars and odd glyphs.

"Check that out," Sharon's voice was muffled to the point that I thought I had water in my ear.

We moved into the room. The floor was clean, painted stark black, a series of constellations etched in marker, like walking on a demented sky. I didn't remember much from my college astronomy classes, so I couldn't judge the accuracy, but someone had clearly spent quite a bit of time on it. I started filming, panning around to catch the whole mural, the way it bled up onto the walls, all of it leading to the main act. In the corner, an antique radio sat on a crooked end table. The case was open, tubes exposed. Wires splayed out from the back into a hallucinatory spider web pattern on the wall, running over the top of the tags and graffiti. That meant they had been placed fairly recently. A pile of translucent plastic loops was tangled on the floor in the corner, like a purple and blue tumbleweed. I gently prodded one with my toe. There were lines etched into the plastic in perfect stripes. In front of the radio, the base of a microphone stand, rusted and covered in flaking green paint.

In the other corner was a camping chair that still looked to be in decent shape. On the floor in front of the chair was a battered spiral notebook filled with diagrams, things hastily scrawled, notes about the cracked sky, refractions, sound travel, frequencies.

I flipped to the front of the book, noting the thick column of shredded paper trapped in the spiral. All of the early notes had been torn out. The first page was dated over a decade ago, starting midway through a journal entry about other hotspots around the sea. The handwriting and charts became more agitated with each turn of the page, losing coherence. A few pages from the end, the scrawl turned childlike, reading:

. . . they want to talk, you understand? They have things to say. Years and years and years. It's important. We are vessels. We were vessels. We opened it and I

wanted nothing to do with it, but now it's open. They cracked it without thinking of what might be on the other side. I never wanted any of it. None of us did, but I'm the one who was cursed to see it. I miss my wife. All of her. Every one of her from every when. I've seen them. I still do. They came through and I never saw them. I only heard them. All of the changes, all of it, it's all them. All them. There is no more. DB? Why? Why DB? What does that mean?

The rest of the pages were hurried slash marks made with a black pen. The back of the last sheet was an endless spiral that looked like the author was trying to get all of the ink out of his pen. Near the top a bloody fingerprint glowed, a dull brown star dying in the void. Or maybe it was just dirt and my mind was giving way to fantasy.

"Holy shit," Sharon pulled the photo out again, comparing it to the handwriting. "What in the honest hell, Dee?"

"I don't know. I don't know, but I'd say we have a story here, wouldn't you?"

"Yeah, but . . . shit. This means we have to stay. We have to, right? We at least need to try turning our radios on." The corners of her jaw worked. I thought she might be biting her lip the way she did when she got frustrated. I wish that's all it had been. She yelped. "Shit! Bit my cheek." She reached up to pull her dust mask off.

"Hey, hey, hey. Let's go outside for a minute, make some plans in the fresh air." I grabbed her hand.

She turned and bumped into me, her attention drawn by something outside the window. "A crack in everything. That's how the light gets in."

We both had a thing for Leonard Cohen. Seemed appropriate given the circumstances, but I should have asked her what she saw. Instead, we walked down the stairs in silence. Maybe it wasn't silence. Maybe she was talking the whole time. Maybe she'd always been talking and I never heard her. How fitting.

BENEATH THE SALTON SEA

We stopped by the camera in the parking lot. I lifted my mask. She did the same, spitting out a gob of bloody saliva. "Really tagged it. Least it's easier to breathe out here."

The stink of the Salton Sea tinged the air, still a refreshing improvement over the dank interior. I checked the camera, fast forwarding through the footage to see if anything interesting had happened while we were inside. It was a still life. Would things be different now if I had also listened to the video? I erased the file and reset the whole thing, checking the battery.

"We can get about four hours out of this thing on low quality video. Probably need to come outside to check the battery once or twice, maybe change out cards. We could set up your camera here on time lapse, maybe one photo every thirty seconds, just in case there's a light show at some point and—"

She grabbed my face and kissed me deeply. Her tongue tasted of blood and salt and something electric. I'd been ready to leave. Hoping she would have started trying to talk me out of this as soon as we got outside. She pulled back and beamed at me.

"I'm sorry I was such a butt earlier. This has been a pretty decent vacation."

I smiled at her. "Let me see your cheek."

"No! It's fine, it'll stop bleeding in a second. Sorry, I got a little excited."

We spent the next few minutes staying busy by the car, me setting up the cameras while Sharon dug out every piece of audio equipment she could find. We had a couple of old mp3 players that also had built-in FM radios. I put a fresh set of batteries in my trusty blue player and jammed it in my pocket, leaving the voice recorder running. The audio might not be great but at least it would be a consistent record. I had an emergency flashlight in the trunk with an AM/FM radio on it and a hand crank. That

21

would last us all night. I brought in a MiniDV camcorder and Sharon came in with an omni-directional microphone plugged into her voice recorder.

We stopped at the entrance to the Yacht Club, the sun fading and the temperature dropping.

"This is dumb, right?" she asked.

"Yep. Very dumb. Still more exciting than talking to a bunch of squatters out in the desert about their opposition to well water and property taxes."

Sharon sighed. "All right. Let's do it. This one's for Doreen."

We walked back up the stairs side-by-side and stepped into the Yacht Club. I looked back at the car as we entered and a ripple moved across the sky, like the end of a film reel flapping against the light. This time it was more clearly defined, like fogged glass in a lightning shape that curved around the mountains and over our heads. I nudged Sharon to look, and she nodded. I snapped a picture. When we checked the frame on the back of the camera, the sky looked perfectly normal.

Nothing about the Salton Sea is normal if you look closely. The sand isn't sand. Just piles and piles of desiccated bones. From a distance, it fools you into thinking of pristine white shores. Up close, you're ankle-deep in razor-sharp fragments of calcified fish parts and bird skeletons. Death surrounds the sea. There are little pockets where life clings on, birds, reptiles, people. It's an ecosystem of living things that rely on other living things too stubborn to leave. Life forcing itself on death, or maybe the other way around.

We went back into the lobby. As soon as we crossed the threshold, a low rumble shot through the room, then a sustained hum, followed by a loud pop like a set of concert speakers coming to life. You ever plug in an electric guitar? That buzz? That crackle? Multiply that by a thousand. We instinctively ducked as the lights snapped on. I looked at

Sharon, her chest moving quickly, the hairs on her arm standing up. Not every fixture was lit, but enough that the room was thrown into a greater level of detail. I almost preferred having the lobby dark.

"Guess we get to save on batteries for a while, huh?"

Sharon nodded and we turned the crank on the emergency radio, bringing it to life. We tried both ends of the dial, finding only a few weak country music broadcasts. At the high end, there was a little bit of an ebb and flow to the static hiss, an undulating rhythm like waves coming in that probably meant nothing, but we stayed with it for a while, staring at the speakers like we'd see sound flowing out.

Sharon headed for the hallway. "Wanna try the old timey radio upst—"

The lights in the building flickered and the air shot through with a sharp static noise like a giant set of lungs taking a deep breath. Then came dreadful silence. It wasn't until a few seconds later that I realized the pounding I heard was my own heartbeat. We held our breath, waiting for the exhale. Waiting for an intonation, an invocation, a whisper, a word.

Nothing.

"What was—" Sharon's jaw dropped.

The lights dimmed and the static returned in regular pulses, a sharp inhale every thirty seconds. As much as my mind tried to rationalize it as *just a noise*, I couldn't help but think of the sound as *breathing*. Only inhaling. The lack of exhale, the absence of that release of pressure spiking my heart rate.

"Is that coming out of the radio?" Sharon asked.

I quickly flipped the switch and checked that all of our gear was off. I scanned the ceiling for old speakers leftover from when the building was still alive, but there was nothing.

Sharon's eyes went wide. She smacked my shoulder

and extended her arms, turning in a slow circle. "You feel that? Stick your hands out. Do it! Move your fingers."

I reached out like a mindless puppet, my fingers brushing through the air, pushing against waves of static that felt like the aura that would buzz around an old CRT TV screen after you shut it off. There was a phrase written in that notebook upstairs, a note about the rising tide. We needed to get back up there.

"It's moving! Hold your fingers still, you can feel it running through . . . "

And I could. Like gritty water flowing through my fingers.

Blackout.

Sharon ran for the door, the last remnants of the setting sun our only guide. Quiet would imply a purposeful lack of sound. This was disorienting, I could only hear our breath, and that was fading as a strange pressure built in my ears. The lights snapped back on and the static/breath noise returned, this time barely audible, high-pitched. It was desperate, like someone breaking the surface of the ocean after a near drowning. Neither of us moved. We looked to one another, hoping for answers, hoping for sense, finding only that same empty anxiety staring back.

"Are we getting any of this?"

Sharon's face lit up and she laughed. "All work and no play. Shit." She fumbled with a couple of her recorders and flipped them on, checking the screen. "Needle's not moving, but we might as well leave it running. I'll go up and check the radio. You check the camera out in the lot and then come find me."

I took half a step toward the door and paused. Sharon laughed again.

"This isn't a scary movie, Dee. Just a creepy abandoned building. Nobody's here but us fishes." She threw her arms around me and pressed her forehead against mine. "This is the worst vacation rental you've ever taken me to. I'm leaving such a shitty Yelp review!"

I gave her a puzzled smile in return. I could smell her skin, the ghost of her soap, her hair. I'd give anything to have that back, just that.

"Check the camera. Go! Shit's happening!" She hustled away, her footsteps strangely silent on the stairs. She stopped halfway up and pulled out her camera. "You stay there. You stay *right* there. Just like that. I want to remember this. I'm going . . . to . . . never forget this."

The flash pulsed hard twice in the gloom, blinding me. And then she was gone.

The clumsiness of her last sentence, like she'd tripped over her own tongue. I hate to think of that now. It's only now as I write this that I recall the purple behind my eyelids. Not the usual stars you get from a flash going off. These were odd, geometric fractals, honeycomb shapes that danced and moved. As far away as I was, there was no way that photo would turn out, and she'd know that.

I got the cold-water-down-my-neck feeling of my fight-or-flight . . . well, just *flight* instinct. I started counting to twenty. Enough time that Sharon would think I'd gone outside to check the gear. Whatever she was feeling, I wasn't getting the same vibe. I wanted to leave. All this strangeness, if it happened once, it would happen again. We could come back with more gear. Better gear. A bigger crew.

. . . and twenty. Every step a tiny mountain. I got to the top of the stairs and looked down the hallway. Dull light pulsed out of the radio room.

"Sharon?"

"Dee? Dee? Dee? I can't see. I can't see. I need a flashlight. Mine died."

I hurried into the radio room, but it was empty.

"See? Dee? See?"

"Sharon, where are you?"

"I'm in it. We're in it. They're here."

Her voice came from the speaker on the old-timey behemoth on the table. The stand in front of the radio was somehow whole again. Five feet tall, a weird round microphone on top.

"This isn't the time to fuck around with the equipment, Sharon. Where are you?"

I moved out into the hallway, anger overtaking fear.

"Deeeeeeeeeeee?" Her voice echoed from the radio room.

I stomped from one room to the next. Layers of odd graffiti and tags curved on the walls and converged near a door at the end of the hallway, as if the art was slowly being pulled inside. Maybe it had been a break room in a past life. The skeleton of an old fridge loomed in the corner, filthy cabinetry and pipes exposed through shattered walls. Sharon stood against the back wall, arms splayed, her paper mask moving so fast it looked like she was chewing gum. Silent.

I was across the room before I even realized I was moving. I pulled the mask from her face. Her breath came out in silent cold puffs. Her mouth jabbered soundlessly, spittle flying.

She needs to see this.

I don't know why that was my first instinct. I fumbled for the MiniDV to start shooting. The screen flickered twice and then stayed blue, the word REC flashing in the corner.

REC REC REC WRECK WRECK

The speakers kicked on and I finally heard her, faintly, a cacophony of words and sounds coming too fast to comprehend. Some words that got repeated more than others, but nothing I'll ever be able to make sense of. Layers of pleading, anger, pity, my name mixed among it all, the only buoy I could cling to. I could pick out words on either side of my name.

Sands. Yuma. White Sands. Delta six three . . .

Breathe. Majesty. Echo. Majesty. Cross. Eternity. The gate, the gate, the gate . . .

She seized my hand. I choked back a tiny scream. She'd pulled her mask on. In the fading light, her eyes were all-pupil, harsh black against the whites. Tiny red veins squirmed and swam like parasites next to her pupils, leaking ink-like into the whites.

"What's wrong, Dee?" This wasn't a question, more that she was begging for an explanation.

"Let's get outside. Are you okay to walk? This has gotten a little too big for us, I think. Don't be scared."

" . . . why should I be scared? Are we okay? Why should I be scared?" The way her eyes searched mine. Like she was out to sea, like I was the thin lifeline tying her to a rescue boat in a black tide.

"Come downstairs." I took her hand, and it felt like I was pulling a balloon behind me.

The lights in the building flickered yellow. She was next to me, her hand in mine, and I could barely see her even though it wasn't dark.

"You feel it?" I extended my fingers and slowly waved my hand around below my knee, like trawling through still water. That gritty sand feeling returned, tingling every nerve up to my wrist. My mind raced back to what we'd had to drink the previous night, the lunch Doreen packed us. Those hippies could have slipped us anything. Psychedelics. Psychoactives. Psychos. Was I about to lose my shit with her? Was I already?

Sharon waved her hand and nodded. "Tickles my feet. Did you see it open?" I hadn't even noticed she'd taken off her shoes and socks.

Every breath I took felt like inhaling liquid sand, tickling my tongue on the way in and rasping my throat when I exhaled. The weird breathing noise started again, this time in reverse, a great exhalation of static hiss that reduced to a bare whisper. I descended the stairs slowly and carefully, making sure Sharon wasn't going to stumble, scanning ahead for rusty nails and sharp objects. *Sharon, where are your shoes?* became a mantra on every step, a way I could make sure she was still there. She wouldn't answer.

By the time we reached the bottom, the exhalation grew quieter, the lights dimmer. Eventually, we were left in darkness. I felt Sharon's hand tug twice, then her fingers slipped through mine.

"Sharon?" I marveled at the electric charge her whispered name shot between my teeth.

"Dee?" Her voice came from the flashlight/radio clenched in my other hand. I didn't remember turning it back on. Across the room, translucent in the dull yellow beam, I saw her silhouette. Standing still and looking, I think, in my direction.

The radio crackled twice. "Are you tired yet?"

"Just come over here and talk to me. We're gonna get outside to the parking lot. I think we need to call it a night. Sleep it off in the car and get home. Okay? Sharon?"

"I'm almost home. It's opening," She took two steps in my direction. A deep, loud *crack* punched beneath my feet, the floor buckling like a shaken rug.

"We can't do this anymore. This is it—"

Another *crack*, this one twice as hard, like someone had sledgehammered the floor from beneath. I tried to shine the flashlight in her direction again, but the bulb had dimmed to nothing. I grabbed for the MiniDV and fumbled it, heard it clatter into the blackness.

"Dee?"

Another *crack*. And another. Her head tottered back and forth. She hunched suddenly and came forward, like she was trying to run.

"Dee? Dee!"

What happened next? The car crash. That's the only way I can describe it. Impact. Pure force that knocked me onto my butt, and when I found my bearings, she was gone. I couldn't move. I thought maybe there was a hole in the floor. Maybe she'd fallen through. Maybe she was out cold in the basement, bleeding to death. But this place wouldn't have a basement. I crawled, slapping at the floor with my free hand, clutching the flashlight/radio in the other like it was my lifeline, screaming her name. Twice my hands splattered into some unidentifiable mess that I hoped was only bird shit or wet paper. No hole in the floor, I was certain of it.

"Sharon? Sharon, please say something."

The static crested for a second, and there was an exchange, two men's voices, nasally, brief, curt. I heard a name, some numbers. Sounded like mission control. I couldn't make out any of the words.

Ahead, the night sky bled through the seam of the great plywood front doors. I pushed forward until I felt the warped wood and punched it. The door swung open easily. What little difference it made in the light ended about three feet into the building.

That Cohen lyric Sharon said earlier echoed in my mind, unmistakably painted above me. The sky . . . was cracked.

A crack in everything, that's how the light gets in . . .

A razor thin tear started somewhere over the horizon and bent at impossible angles, backtracking against itself until it looped down behind the sea, like some manic god had slashed the sky with a knife in a fit of jealous rage. It bled light into the purple void, an inky flow of indigo-black. There were no stars. No moon. I stumbled out and looked for the car, banging my knee on the tripod we'd set up earlier. I slapped at my pockets for the keys. If I could shine the headlights into the doorway, maybe . . . but Sharon had the keys.

I had to get help. I looked around for any sign of movement nearby, on the road, anything. There was no life out here.

But in the sea!

In the Salton Sea, the placid sea, all of the stars shone, and the moon. I looked up again to a black sky, then back at the water. I didn't realize I'd taken off my shoes until I felt the cold mud between my toes, a sock still on my left foot. I ignored every prick and cut from the bone shards on the beach until I felt my legs enter the water. Knee-deep, I turned to the Yacht Club. A dark silhouette up in one of the windows, a person, a woman, maybe. I hoped it was Sharon. Had to be. She hadn't fallen through the floor, that was just an overactive imagination. *Scare-Dee Cat*, Sharon used to tease me.

I didn't want to run. I didn't want this to end. I just wanted her next to me for this. I was standing in the sky, swimming in the stars and the moon and the endless black! None of it mattered if she wasn't here.

Sharon.

I shouted her name until her voice came over the radio still clutched in my hand.

"Where did you go, Dee?"

"I'm outside! Can you make it? Are you okay? I want you to see this. Come out! Look down at the sky! Look!"

"If you knew this was the last thing I'd ever tell you, what would you want me to say?"

"Why? No, Sharon. Just come outside and see this!"

"I know how to open the gate. They'll show us everything, but we have to pay first. We have to give them—*zzzxxxzzz* . . . " Static swallowed her voice.

Then the voices came. First there were only two. They were children. Shouting and playing. Speaking a language I'd never heard, something ancient and guttural. There was an undercurrent of that same static-breath noise, but this time much more organic. Alive, pulsating, breathing at regular intervals. Each inhale weighed me down, sank me slightly deeper into the mud. Every time it exhaled, I could feel it sliding through the hairs on my arms, tugging my wrist toward the sea.

When I was thigh-deep, a chill rushed through my skull, poured over my spine, and spread across my limbs. I needed to connect with Sharon. I somehow knew it would happen through the sea. Something was between us. I stripped down to my underwear, convinced the heat from the reflected stars would keep me safe. I should have been freezing, but I was fine. Warm. Relaxed. I was in my body and in the water at the same time.

There were things in the sea. Beyond the curling, sun-dried remains of thousands of tilapia stirred up by my footsteps, long, leathery, undulating things moved past my legs. Not seaweed, not here. When I looked down, I saw my naked legs plunging into an impossibly starry night sky. When I moved my feet, the stars swam away from me like ducks. Waves of vertigo washed over me, I wasn't sinking. I was melting. I would become unrooted and sink into the sky.

I looked to the Yacht Club. There she was, on the shore, her skin pale and radiant in the reflected starlight. "I don't want to get my feet muddy, Dee. Come over here." She extended a hand. "I figured it out. They helped me see what's between us. Between everything. You just have to stop talking so that they can start. You just—"

Blood poured from her mouth in a thick, gurgling stream. It mixed with spittle, spattering down onto the muddy ground as she tried to talk. Her eyes went wide in panic. She was sinking, the muck around the shore slowly swallowing her up. I tried to rush to her, nightmare-slow slogging through the silt. She was hip-deep by the time I fought my way back to shallow water. The water felt jello-thick. Things below grabbed and scratched at my ankles. I stumbled, falling to my knees. I pressed up and lunged for her, falling again, my face slapping through the foul water to crack against a rock. I inhaled a mouthful of thick, rancid water and then the ground parted. I shouldn't have been able to see in the brackish mess, but there was a hole

31

in the sea bed. There was another night sky below. Not a sky. *Lights.* Southern California, all of it, dazzling, spinning dizzily beneath me.

I tried to push up out of the water, afraid of drowning, afraid of falling, afraid of losing Sharon forever. I punched through the muck into that sub-sky. Clumps of mud and filthy water spun away through the air, sailing down to splatter the ground miles below. It was such an odd sensation, feeling the current of the water around me, rushing over me, none of it pouring through the hole beneath me. The sea bed under my fingers solidified. I kept my eyes closed and pumped my legs until my face slid and scraped against the grit of the mud near the shore. I squirmed and writhed and pushed until cold air stung my back. I dragged myself from the water, primordial, screaming, spitting water, hacking coughs.

Sharon was gone.

There was a disturbance in the mud at the shoreline, bloodstained splats across the ground like demented graffiti. Sharon's hiking shoe lay a few feet away, caked in dirt, a curled tilapia carcass glued to the muck on the sole. Her headband stuck half-out of the mud, surrounded by small puddles of brown-red water.

Tiny fires raged across my face, my hands, my forearms; razor-slices from rocks and bones, agitated by salt and filth and blood. I dragged myself toward the Yacht Club, dizzy and reeling. The night was black, but I saw everything vibrating in crystal detail. A chorus sang in the sky, endless voices and static, screams and songs and sounds I'd never heard before or since. The building bled cyan and magenta and indigo light from every open crack and window. A shape passed by the window upstairs again, silhouettes surrounded by strange fractals of light. A man and a woman, fighting. Or dancing?

I made my way inside. Some light fixtures had come back, casting painful shades of reds and blues. I wondered what would happen if I had those old-style 3D glasses. No hole in the floor. No Sharon. I went upstairs, treading carefully across the splintered floor, trying to avoid the trash and debris from broken walls and windows. I rubbed a sand-covered palm across my bare shoulder, bringing pain; tried to dust my hands off on my naked thighs, but it felt like rubbing broken glass. I should have found my shoes in the mud before coming inside. When I reached the top of the landing, the radio crackled down the hall. A whisper scraped by my ear. Maybe it was Sharon. Could you identify a loved one by their whisper?

"Did we talk enough? Did we? Was this a mistake? All of this?"

"No! No mistake. We weren't. This wasn't."

A hum rose from the wall, pitches ranged in perfect fifths, a brassy, brutal harmony. I pushed on, ignoring the broken glass stabbing into my feet, the chill in my bones. My skin had become numb. I pounded my arms against my chest to try to get my blood flowing. My bra and underwear looked like sand carvings etched into my skin. I ran my fingers through my hair and found it soaked, caked in mud. My face was covered in gritty silt and dust.

"Help," I whispered. "Sharon. I'm sorry. We have to go, baby. We have to leave."

The doorway to the radio room bled dull orange light into the hallway like a fog, obscuring more than it revealed. I stopped at the doorframe and leaned my head in. The radio was lit up like Christmas, the antenna lines that spread across the wall burning with strange energy. The mural painted on the floor glowed harsh white. It had changed from a starry sky to a thin, weaving line that ran a circuit around the length of the room and spiraled inward to form a circle in front of the radio.

The microphone stand was gone. Sharon was on her knees in the center of the circle, facing away from me. She looked like a religious icon, surrounded by an aura of twisted wires.

"We should have talked," her voice came through the radio. "We could have talked. Why didn't we talk?"

Her shoulders heaved. I limped toward her.

She snapped an arm out to her side. "Don't come closer. It's too late now. Just leave. I don't want you to see."

"See what, baby?" My voice was raw sandpaper. "See what? Sharon, what's happening right now?"

"Everything they wanted," the radio said. "Everything they ever wanted. We opened the door without thinking about what was on the other side. They just want it closed, but first we have to go away. All of us. Every single one. They are very, very angry with us . . . "

"Sharon, look at me. Please."

A wet slap in the dirt near my feet as something small and damp ricocheted across the top of my foot, painting a streak across the muddy brown before tumbling through the dust and filth between my feet. Dark. A lump of meat jiggled on the floor against the edge of my big toe. Sharon rose and the lights in the room grew brighter. No. It was the pattern in the floor, glowing. She turned, tight and confined as if there was an invisible wall surrounding the circle. Her head was down, hair hanging wild as she regarded her bloody fingers.

"Please look at me, Sharon." My jaw chattered, from cold, from fear.

She looked up. A scream—rooted deep in my stomach, through my core, into the floor, the center of the earth—shattered my parched throat. Her chin was black with coagulating blood. Her bottom lip looked like an animal had been chewing on her face. Her left eye was deep purple and shiny, not a bruise. Just milky and iridescent. Her right eye bled indigo light. In one hand she held her bloody knife. She brought her other hand up, two fingers tapping on her chin as she smiled at me.

34

"It was the only way they would listen. The only way to make you hear," the radio said, static tearing her voice. Her lips didn't move. She smiled, an awful, gaping thing that sent rivulets of bloody saliva cascading down her chin and chest. She flicked out her tongue, what was left of it. It looked like a lumpy meatball between her teeth.

"What's happening, Sharon? What's happening?"

"You tell me."

"There's light everywhere. The sky was in the sea, and the real sky was black. Everywhere I look I see light. I see the cracks."

"And do you hear them?"

"I just hear noise. Songs and screams and whispers."

"All I see is the dark, but I can hear them perfectly."

"Them? Who?"

"I'm okay. It's all in pieces. You see the light everywhere? I can't. I only hear them. Together we can make it work. Let them use your eyes. This is the last thing we do together." She smiled and extended the knife toward me. She raised her eyebrows in that same way she used to do when she'd surprise me with an anniversary present. Shit, was that today?

"Give them your eyes and you'll see everything." She came forward, not threatening, just earnestly holding that blade up like this all made perfect sense.

"Lance Corporal Raymond Wood. He was here when it opened. He listened to them and he tried to see them and speak to them and it was too much. But together . . . Maybe together we can . . . "

She walked over to the window. The sky outside was flat, burnt orange. No stars, no moon, no rising sun.

"I can't," I whispered. "I can't. What did you do, Sharon? *What did you do?*"

Sharon dropped the knife and held her hand out to me. "I always followed you. You never had to ask. I just wanted to be there with you. Follow me."

"What did you do?" My hands shook as I raised them to her face. She closed her eyes and nuzzled her cheeks into my palms, her blood still hot and sticky on her chin.

"I always wanted you to know. I was *zzzxzxzx* . . . –ou." A burst of static overrode her voice. "You wer—*xxzzzxzxz*—for me, but *zxzzzzzzz*—and you only had to say it. You only had to say *zzzzzxxxxx* . . . " The volume on the radio dropped. The lights in the room faded and the speaker gave out a final sputter before popping once and humming faintly.

Sharon slid her stained hands up my bare arms, leaving streaks of her blood until she held my face in her hands. Our foreheads touched, I looked into her eyes, watching the unnatural blues and purples fade, her pupils dilated and pulsed until her eyes were almost black. Her mouth went slack and she let out a soft sigh.

"Sharon?"

She didn't move.

I pressed my lips against hers, ignoring the tang of blood, the shredded lips, willing my breath into her. The room grew colder. I shook, the lack of clothing finally catching up to me. Sharon swayed on her feet, her skin losing color, eyelids fluttering.

An explosion of static blasted from the radio in the corner. It grew louder and louder until it filled the room, no longer an exhale or inhale but a sustained scream threatening to shred my eardrums.

My knees knocked together and my breath came in hitching rasps. I put my arm around Sharon's shoulder and pressed myself into her, leading her forward, out of the room. I briefly considered picking up the lump of her tongue from the floor. It was no use. It was just bloody meat now, speckled in plaster chips and sawdust. I'd never hear her voice again, never see that tongue stick out when she was concentrating, never feel it brush my neck, kiss me deeply. How much of us is our voice? How much of ourselves can we lose before we become something else?

We staggered down the stairs and through the lobby. Platinum-gold beams of light sliced through the gap in the front doors. I pushed one open, expecting headlights, or the police, or even a bonfire, but not the rising sun. Night was just starting when we went inside a few hours ago. The car was locked. I dumbly patted my bare hips, searching for keys in pockets that weren't there. Sharon's pockets were empty. Every step felt like a marathon but only carried us a few inches. If I could get us to the road, we'd have a chance. The cold had eaten me through to my core. I looked down at my feet, sliced and bloody and stuck through with thousands of fish bones. Sharon was near catatonic.

Get to the road. Someone will see us, someone will find us, help will come, or we will die.

Words raced through my mind. Hypothermia. Fear. Failure. Death. Divorce. Armageddon. Love? Where was love? Why wasn't love there? I didn't know what else to do, so I walked.

The tripod that held our camera was at the edge of the lot, so I picked it up and used it as a cane. I walked until I couldn't. I got us to the median of Grapefruit Boulevard and then my legs just wouldn't move anymore. I took Sharon by the hands and gently pulled her down next to me. I sat cross-legged in the middle of the eastbound lane and leaned her head into my lap. In the sun, she looked terrifying. Her skin was robin's-egg-blue, lips dried and cracked, her face coated with blood.

Here in the light I noticed odd shapes carved into her arm. Glyphs and symbols that could have been a map or a message or just mutilation. My vision started going grey at the edges and I leaned my head against hers. I wanted to whisper to her, all of the things I'd wanted to say for so many years and stupidly kept buried. The good, the bad, all of it. My voice was broken. Breathing took effort. I tried to tap my fingers on her wrist, this little gesture we used to make at the movies to remind each other that we were there, close, in the silent dark.

I rolled my head back to see the crack in the sky, clear as day, sharp as permanent marker on glass. It wasn't a crack at all. It was a design, geometric, orderly symbols that almost matched the ones on Sharon's arms.

My vision left. The asphalt felt like a gentle river beneath me, carrying us. I heard the roar of an approaching engine, downshifting, tires biting into gravel. Then shouting. I disappeared somewhere into the blackness of my mind, where everything was quiet and the inside of my brain was painted with the endless sea of stars that should have been in the sky that night.

They found one of our voice recorders during the investigation. I've reviewed the audio countless times. It's just static, with a high-pitched whine in places that may have been an odd frequency or maybe Sharon's screams. The only surviving footage on the camera from the lot was when I ran from the Yacht Club the first time. Hours of nothing, and then something hits the camera from the side. I'm pretty sure it was me, wobbling off to the sea. Twenty minutes later, from a skewed angle, my naked, mud-smeared legs walk past the camera. Somewhere around forty minutes after that, there's a brief movement near the corner of the building. Shadows pass by the upstairs window. It's too grainy to confirm if it's one person or two, man or woman. They assume it's us, but I'm not sure. They found a crumpled military hat in the mud beneath the window. It looked to be from the mid 1950s. Nobody could agree on whether it had just been placed there or was dug up. It was negative on hair and skin samples. Inside the Yacht Club, they found syringes, spent bags of powder and empty pill bottles. Five different knives. Three of them had dried blood on the blade, none of them matched Sharon.

No amount of reconstructive surgery could give back her tongue. It wouldn't matter because she hadn't tried to communicate with anyone since the EMTs brought her back. I have dreams every year on this day, the same as the fever dreams I had when they found us by the roadside the next day, near-hypothermic.

We spent a week recovering in the hospital before the detectives came. They questioned us for days, convinced that we'd been kidnapped, drugged, and tortured. They started building that narrative while we slept and did their damnedest to get us to confirm their worst suspicions. The first time the detective suggested it, I spat in his face. The second time, I stopped talking to them. They tried getting Sharon to write a deposition, but she was catatonic.

They eventually settled on a diagnosis of hallucinations based on toxoplasmosis. They said we'd spent so many hours inhaling powdered bird shit that it snapped something in our brains. They didn't bother to test the empty water bottle Doreen had given us. I didn't want them to.

That was as close to famous as we got. The first year, we were ridiculed in the media as a pair of crackpot hippie lesbians who got lost on a drug adventure. The years after that, nobody but the conspiracy theorists would talk to us. There were a few out there who'd heard Doreen's tall tale. I wanted nothing to do with them. I returned to Slab City twice to find Doreen, but she was nowhere to be found. Nobody would talk to me. They'd seen me on the news. Thought I just wanted to bleed more sensationalist stories out of them.

I went back to Bombay Beach years later. The black line in the sand was gone. The Yacht Club got its much needed renovation, reopening as the glorious Salton Sea History Museum. I kept my head down the whole time I was there, though there was nobody to hide from. I couldn't bring myself to go inside. Instead, I walked down to the shore and stared at the sky until I was dizzy.

This year will be the last that I go to visit Sharon. I brought in a print of that selfie we took in the desert, her silly smile, the nervous energy on our faces, and tears started pouring down her cheeks. She looked at me then, really saw me for the first time in I don't know how long, and it was nothing but hatred. She pounded on that photo with her finger, hitting the same spot in the background over and over: the sea.

So, we're going to drive back to the sea, and we're going to wade in. I'm going to take Sharon to the sky beneath the Salton Sea, show her the stars, the world below our world. I'm going to get it all back. The singing, the sound, her voice, us, all of it. There's nothing left for us here. What broke us once will make us whole again. I'm going to find the crack in everything and shatter it, blow it wide open, dive through.

Last night, I dreamed of the last page of that journal we found in the Yacht Club, that page of spirals that I was certain were the scribblings of a madman. He wasn't trying to bleed the ink from his pen. He was trying to draw the stars below the waves. It was a map for anyone brave and insane enough to follow.

If you're looking, here is where you'll find us.

April 9, 1949–
April ∞, 1956

I sent Doreen a letter explaining in exacting detail what was going to happen, and when, and why she should get on the first train heading east even though there would never be a train

heading far enough east for it to matter. East was here as much as here was here. I told her to run. Just in case my math was wrong. Maybe the sky wasn't about to tear in half but something was about to happen. She might survive it, but I'd never see her again. But I'd never stop seeing her. Forever. Maybe give her a chance to survive even a second longer in the world we knew before. They were going to turn the machine on, and the sky would change. Tactical application, that was their rallying cry. I knew. I knew the machine could never be turned off. That, in truth, there was no machine. The device was like a railyard switch. The tracks were going one way, and when the switch was flipped, the tracks would turn and lead to a different path, while the train still ran on top. The train was always on top, always running. That was the worst of it. We are here, and soon, we will be there, and very few people will see what happened, and those that do will never

understand it. Failing that, we will cease to exist. It's not an on/off switch, it's a single push of a button to decide: different or destroyed?

I outlined all of it to her in a five-page letter. I took excruciating pains to get that letter off base. The next day, I found the letter on my

desk with a photo portrait of Doreen attached to every page, torn in half, each half stapled through the neck. Broken apart. They

viewed this as a threat, but I knew it was what would

happen either way. They could threaten her, even kill her, but will it matter when the machine turns on? Will she not be murdered here and living there, missing me in either location? Thinking beyond binary, will she not exist infinitely across all whens and nows and thens and heres and theres? Will she not be dead or deranged or destroyed or damaged in each of those, and will the only constant be the lack of my presence? If I found my way back to her, find my way back, to any of the infinite Doreens, will that close a loop? Will the train only run on one track again? Or does it only mean that I will see the singular track instead of all of them?

They came for me later that day, after I found my letter to Doreen returned and altered, insisting some urgent work needed to happen on the machine. They dragged me from my room in the barracks and out into the hot California sun. I didn't resist, but I didn't walk either. I knew where they were taking me, and I knew what would happen, because the machine had shown it to me in the future. The machine had made me infinite and endless, and I saw everything in my life, in my *lives*, front to back and all around. Now was then and then was now.

I let my weight sag, the tips of my boots describing twin arcs in the gravel and dirt between the barracks and the jeep they tossed me into. I asked them to look at the ground, told them, that's

the sky, that will be the sky. I told them they shouldn't do what they were about to do, but it was done already. They bore no guilt.

They sat me before the machine. They told me something was out of alignment. I

was the only one who knew how to fix it. I'm writing this letter to you, Doreen, two weeks before I'll write that other letter explaining that day, everything, one week after they dragged me away, I'm writing it

while the sky breaks and I'm writing it while I enlist in the special division. I'm writing it from the

stratosphere, seeing American ambition rend the sky and suck entire cities into the void of space, and I'm writing it from below the ground, when we shelter as the machine fails. All I have to do is keep writing. I am the constant. I am the stitch holding everything together. Holding us inside, holding them back. They're interested in us. That's the worst part, the part that should scare the hell out of everyone. Not that they want to cross over, not that they are going to come through, that they are interested in us. In so many ways. They will watch. If we time this right, if we do this right, we can close it all. People will get hurt, but they're going to get hurt anyway. We need to find hurt people. You'll know them when you see them. You can offer them anything. I'm telling you this, standing next to your bed as you sleep, or weeks before I enlisted in the armed forces, or the night before I first asked you to the sock hop in high school. I'm speaking to you now and always, because death isn't the end. That's the only thing I've discovered, but it's been a terrible revelation, knowing. The knowing of every instance of everything. Understanding possibility, probability, sifting certainty from any uncertainty, seeing every possible end at once. But you can draw me back. It will be late in the day as the sun sinks. Or late in your life. I will look just as you remembered me. Stand by the sea. Remember where we sat watching birds, before the water turned, before everything died. This will be later, but before the sea dries out. Before the lakebed turned to crystal, sunbaked and powdered and airborne and weaponized. Before everything dies. I have to reach you. I can reach you anytime.

But you can only reach me once. It starts here.

First the tide will rise. After sundown. The breeze. Then the birds. Isn't the season for insects, but maybe you'll hear a few. Then you'll grow tired. Then I'll come to you.

If you have visitors, be kind to them. Offer them food and water and kindness. Encourage them to stay. Encourage them to explore. The opening comes in waves, and I'm always so

close. Right next to it, but also separated like I'm on a mountain peak in China and it's in California somewhere. Time and space ripple. Everything here wants to come through. Water wants to find its own level. Tides come and go, and if I can follow one out, maybe, like a riptide, someone else could cross back over. I realize this isn't fair. None of it is fair. It's not going to be fair.

Sometime, probably sixty years after the ink dries on this paper, things will line up just right. I don't want you to be complicit in anything.

You will have a hard time seeing it. Keep your eyes peeled. I remember you used to hate when I said that, said it gave you the creeps. You will misunderstand this later in a way that will make me regret I ever said it. I see it now as inevitable.

When the sky rends—when the sky tore the first time—it's eternal, it happens this way every time because it never stopped happening. We are a groove on an infinite record track, and this is what it's like when we pass below

the needle: There will be a jellyfish, great and arcing and everywhere and everything. It hasn't risen from the sea. It has always been there. It's there now. The crack in the sky isn't a gateway, it is a fracture in the mirror and I've seen behind it and now I understand it's always been there. It's always been there because it is. It just is.

When the sky
mends — when the sky
bore the first crack,
it's eternal, it
happens this way
every time because it
never stopped
happening. We are a
groove on an infinite
record track and
this is what it's like
when we pass below

the needle. There
will be a religion,
great and arcing
and everywhere
and everything. It
hasn't risen from
the sea. It has
always been there.
It's there now. The
crack in the sky
isn't a gateway, it is
a fracture in the
mirror and I've
seen behind it and
now I understand
it's always been
there. It's always
been there because
it is, it just is.

II.

YOUR PERFECT OFFERING

May 2012-May 1987-May 2012

FOUR YEARS AGO, Sharon came back from the Salton Sea missing her tongue. Four years of silence, catatonic. All I wanted was a word from my sister, any word.

If you're looking, here is where you'll find us.

That was the last line in the tiny notebook her wife Dee left on her hospital bed. After four years I hadn't come close to understanding what she'd been through, but I was finally learning to cope.

And now this. Now she was gone again.

There was still debate over whether she bit her tongue off or cut it out. I saw it in my dreams all the time. Hadn't heard a word from her in years, but when I slept . . .

Every day that I could, I'd visit her in the hospital. Something was trapped in her, a memory like a jagged sliver of glass lodged in her throat, too painful to release. Maybe I was just projecting. She was my only family, and I have plenty of living relatives.

After that horrible weekend, Sharon and Dee became minor celebrities, the type of fame that comes from relentless mocking on the internet. They left Los Angeles an anonymous married couple and came back as those two dumb lesbians from the Salton Sea. Four years, an endless torrent of emails, voicemails, requests for interviews, unrequested photos of men's half-wilted erections, stalkers, violent fantasies of what people would do to them if given a chance. And for what?

Sharon's silence was carte blanche for people to project meaning onto her. Every week I'd get DMs on Twitter from fake Sharon accounts. Hell, one of them earned a coveted blue checkmark for a few weeks, they were that convincing. Eventually, the attention subsided, but a trickle of rape threats still feels like a biblical flood. Some of that spilled over onto me, too. I haven't felt safe for years, and Sharon got to be catatonic through it all. Selfishly, I wanted to be there with her. Or I wanted her out here going through it with me.

Fast forward a few years, and Sharon and Dee became forgotten internet lore to all but the hardcore "fans". The crackpots. Because of the video. Creepy establishing shots of the building they'd explored, the abandoned North Shore Yacht Club. Shaky tracking shots in dimly lit hallways, capturing graffiti and scrawled messages on the walls, weird lights, shadows. There was a lot of that grade-Z shit you see on TV ghost hunter shows, where they'd be talking and both suddenly hush, asking if the other had heard something. There's nothing on the video besides them, no sounds but their voices. The video lies.

A small corner of the internet has obsessed over their footage, determined it was evidence of demonic possession. Or alternate planes of existence. Or a dimensional rift. Or aliens. Take your pick, someone out there wanted to believe. In the hours of footage, there are dark rooms with a dull glow in one tiny corner. Whispers. Screaming. Voices. A lot of people bought into the hyper-enhanced audio, the over-pixelated still frames that gave Rorschach-evidence of things that go bump in the night as concrete evidence. I guess I was one of those people. I listened to the podcasts, *Salton Signal*, or *Slab City Skies*. I was a moderator on the *Haunted Roadshow* Reddit. Not because I believed. It was just the fastest way to get information.

I knew every frame of their famous video by heart, the camera they set up outside of the building in the dirt lot. Another inside of the main lobby. The handheld footage. Sharon started the night looking healthy but a little nervous. The last time she appeared in one of the videos, she was pale, a little skittish, like she was on a bad mushroom trip. A different video from outside showed one of them leaving the building, running into the camera. Half-naked, or maybe all naked. I still don't know if it was her or Dee. The camera goes down, and there's a very faint sound of splashing, someone going into the Salton Sea, or maybe coming out. That was all the evidence I had to figure out what happened. Where did I lose her?

I knew where her body was, catatonic in the hospital. Nobody was home. I'd visit and show her old pictures of us, brought her old toys, sang to her, but there was never a spark. She'd cry or moan sometimes, but the doctors said that wasn't unusual for someone in her condition.

And then, two days ago, Dee took her away. I only found out after getting a call from my none-too-distraught father. There were no signs of struggle, just an empty bed with a ragged college-ruled notebook full of lies, and a crude map to where she had taken my sister. Dee wore out a couple of pens on that map, blacking out the whole page, but leaving spots, constellations that didn't exist, a big placid lake below them.

If you're looking, here is where you'll find us.

The night she was taken, I dreamt of stars. I was floating in the Salton Sea, way out in the middle of the water. I couldn't see the shoreline. Couldn't smell the rancid water. It was nice. The sky above me was deep purple, clear, shot through with pinpricks of diamond-bright light. Cliché, yeah, but there's not a better phrase for it. I paddled, and the stars moved with me, circling me, directing me where to go. Sharon was coming out from shore, glowing and golden. Walking toward me, right on top of the water. Calling my name. Over and over, Zuuuula, a gentle cooing, like she used to do when we were kids playing hide and seek. She was six years old before she figured out how to pronounce my name, but Zula stuck for the rest of my life, and only with her. I'd hated that name on everyone's lips except hers. For her, I was Zula. For everyone else, even my parents, I was Susan.

She would sing, *Zula, Zula, I love Zula, she is my stars and moon . . .*

We were all each other had, through all of the family moves, the divorce, the abuse. Our world existed on a different plane, secret lives, secret names, we were always safe if we were together.

She was stepping across the sea, leaving footprints. "See what I saw," she said, sing-speaking, then shouting until it was a scream, a throat-tearing yowl so frightening I swam away from her. She broke into a sprint across the water until she was five feet away, and then it was like she fell off a cliff. She disappeared, a quiet ripple of rings expanding from her final step. I paddled closer to investigate, and she grabbed my ankle, dragging me under.

Beneath the surface, it was daylight, and there was no water. We floated in a bright blue sky, clouds below our feet, the water a ceiling above us. I couldn't breathe. She pawed at me, climbing up my body until her cold, wet hands were on my cheeks. She vomited water, great gouts of brown, brackish filth, until my shirtfront and pants were soaked, until she was coughing. I tried to calm her, but I couldn't breathe. It was like taking water into my lungs. She pulled her face close to mine, her eyes wide and wild, mouth gaping, teeth coated in blood and saliva. Her tongue, what was left of it, an angry red stump of hamburger meat. She wasn't angry. I knew those eyes.

"Find me," she screamed. And I heard it. I swear it was echoing off my walls when I snapped awake. Imagine, just imagine, knowing your sister cried out to you for help and you didn't do a damn thing for two days. How would that make you feel?

And then, nine o'clock the next night my dad called. *Your sister's dyke wife broke her out.*

I instantly hung up on him and spent an entire night trying to talk to someone at the hospital. They told me I had to call back during regular hours the next morning. I called back every thirty minutes until the sun rose, then I drove there to see what had happened. They wouldn't tell me much beyond what they saw in the room. Dee's visit was perfectly fine because she was the spouse, and somewhere in there someone broke protocol, and now they were gone. The notebook was open on that last page, and I burned it into my mind. I'm sure I'd heard most of the stories in that notebook in the intervening years of trying to get Dee to tell me what happened out there, to take even an ounce of responsibility. I eventually stopped caring about the *whys* and only wanted the *who* back. I wanted my Sharon.

Approaching thirty-six hours of no sleep, I slammed two cups of coffee and hit the road, only stopping for gas and to get my hands on as much trucker speed as it took to keep me awake. Hair exploding in every direction, I couldn't tell if my makeup was smeared or just absorbing into my skin.

I didn't call anyone in my family to tell them where I was going, because why would they care? They'd stopped talking about Sharon and her *preferences* as soon as she was in the hospital. Out of sight, out of mind. Might have been the best years of their lives knowing they didn't have a sinner running around SoCal anymore. Between my family's not-so-latent homophobia and the Mayberry-level quality of law enforcement out in the desert, I was the only one I trusted enough to bring her back. The only one left who cared.

I kept to the speed limit, signaling cautiously, coming to a complete stop whenever required. Too paranoid to speed, so paranoid I thought driving normally would be what busted me. I couldn't risk getting pulled over. My trunk was loaded with whatever seemed essential when I left. A warm jacket. Flashlights. Zip ties. A couple of steel pipes. Duct tape. A little souvenir LA Dodgers bat. Whatever it took.

Dee's hand-drawn map from the journal didn't make sense. The geography was wrong, as if someone had asked a child to draw a lake, any lake. But it was a start. It ended at the North Shore Yacht club, so that's where I headed. That building, what was left of it, was the main focus of their videos. It was an absolute hellhole when they'd been there. A once-grand facility that had been gutted and left for dead, its corpse defiled by wildlife and graffiti artists. What the hell could have enticed them to go inside?

There was an old woman mentioned in the journal. All I knew was her name was Doreen and she was a little crazy. I tried to find her a few times over the years, but nobody'd heard of her. At least that's what they said. They protect their own. Doreen enticed them with the idea that there was a crack in the sky above the Salton Sea. That's what they'd been chasing, and over the course of their videos, it seems they thought they'd found it.

I pulled up to the Yacht Club, and it was like stepping into another dimension. I sat in the parking lot, straining, trying to make sense of what I was seeing now versus what they saw. There was fresh vegetation here, green trees, gleaming metal and pristine brick designed to evoke the large ships and bustling times of an era long-dead. It was hot as hell in the parking lot. There were a couple of tourists, and a few bikers taking a break from a desert ride. I dug around on the floor to find my beanie hat, got my hair mostly under control, and stepped out of the car, stretching so hard I popped every bone in my sternum.

I walked around the building's left side, down toward the water, pulling out my phone and opening the saved videos folder. A couple of old brick buildings still stood, the remains of a bait stand and a boat shack. These hadn't gotten the fancy treatment. They were the scars of what Dee and Sharon had seen. The ground was littered with rocks and discarded sun-bleached cans and bottles. Closer to shore, the dirt transitioned into a fine white powder I mistook for sand. Endless tiny bones, crunching underfoot, inches deep. Skeletal remains of birds and fish, spreading out as far as the eye can see, like every creature that ever died had found its way to shore.

See what I saw, she said in the dream.

I shaded the phone with my hand, opening the video I downloaded from the *Haunted Roadshow* Reddit. Dee had set their camera up on a tripod in the lot near the shore, so I paused the video and moved around until I lined up what I saw with what was on the screen. I hit play, hoping the change of location would give me some new perspective. Something splashed in the sea behind me. I glanced back, wondering where Dee fell in, if Sharon's wounds were truly self-inflicted or if she'd been the one to mutilate my sister before diving into the lake.

The longer the video lingered on that establishing shot of the Yacht Club, the lonelier I felt. It was astounding, seeing the beautiful building before me contrasted with the dilapidated remains onscreen. Two different worlds existing simultaneously.

"Here! Here!" one of the bikers in the lot shouted.

They were an older couple, silver-haired weekend warriors, dressed in matching leather one-piece road suits. They held small radios, the woman trying to help the man tune his. I'll be damned, people actually did the radio thing out here just like in Dee's story, chasing phantom transmissions.

A cold breeze cut through me. I looked down just in time to see a naked woman on the screen. My thumb hammered the pause icon. I've watched the scene where the camera gets knocked over thousands of times. I've watched this video, or parts of it, almost daily for years. I've never seen this.

Her hair, wet and tangled, clinging to her face and draping over either shoulder to cover her breasts. Her torso a slick of black, wet blood. Her chest rose slightly, slowly, then faster, and faster, until she was panting, sucking air in, her eyes wide, white, screaming something, blood spraying from her mouth.

This video was paused. She wasn't.

I couldn't tell if it was Dee because her hair was soaked and muddy, blocking most of her face. Was there sound? What was she saying? I turned the volume up, but as soon as I hit the volume rocker, the video hiccupped and she was gone. I rewound and replayed. Nothing. Maybe I'd gone back too far, or not far enough.

I saw her. I saw her. I tried a few more times, getting nothing but the still-life of the old Yacht Club.

"It's happening!" one of the bikers shouted.

"Ssssh!"

I stood a respectful distance away as they huddled around their radios. When one of them let out a whoop, I approached.

"You hear them too, huh?" I asked, pulling a small battery-powered radio from my pocket. It had a neck lanyard, so I slid it on, turning up the volume slightly. I pretended to fiddle with the frequency, anything to keep my head down. If they were aficionados, they might recognize me from the handful of TV interviews I gave regarding the case.

"Yes!" the woman said. "What did you hear?"

"I thought I had something but I must have moved the wrong way. Kinda like fishing, huh? Sounds like you got a big one."

"I got two minutes of it!"

"It's just air traffic, I keep trying to tell her," the man said. "We're right under some major flight paths. And the way the ground is out here, transmissions reflect all over, from—"

"What did you hear?" I asked. "The Ghost Transmissions?" I hated that name, but one of those paranormal TV shows christened the weird radio phenomena people sometimes caught out here and it stuck.

"It was, I don't know, sounded like they were calling in an airstrike. Everything was staticky, but I got a few words," she produced a tiny notebook, "tried to write 'em down. A man's voice. *Mission. Repeat. Echo Echo.* Then two hard blasts of some weird noise."

"That's called a squelch, honey. When I was working ATC in the mil—"

"Then it was *Pelican*," she cut her husband off. "Then bomb bay Zula—"

"Zulu, honey, it's standard—"

"Well, it sounded like Zula to me!" she shushed him. "It said that one a few times, just a second ago. Bomb bay Zula. Three times. It cut off just before you came over."

"Which station?"

"It's . . . I mean I had it on 1240AM, but now there's nothing. Not even static. That's weird, huh?"

"Yeah, weird. Maybe I'll try a different spot. Happy hunting!" I hustled back to the car, hyperventilating. It was cold. Why was it cold? I rolled the window down and sat back, my heart jackhammering. I didn't imagine the woman in the video. I didn't fucking dream that up.

The bikers looked over at me with a start. Did I say that out loud?

"Bomb Bay Zula!" I shouted, giving them a thumbs up. They returned a half-hearted wave. Good enough. They'd write me off as a crazy local.

I consulted my map. Bombay Beach, a twenty-minute drive. I tore open another packet of trucker speed and shook the pills into my mouth, sloshed them down with lukewarm water. I'd moved beyond headache into spine-ache. Everything hurt. Couldn't sleep until I found her.

I slammed back onto the road, kicking up gravel the whole way to Grapefruit Boulevard, the main highway. My eyes danced from the road to the car's thermometer. Steady at seventy-six degrees until I was a mile away from the Yacht Club. The next time I glanced down, two, five, ten minutes later, it said ninety-four. The window turned oppressively hot. It was the pills. The lack of sleep. Everything was fucking with me. Another three temp checks and I was at the exit for Avenue A. Off the highway and back toward the shore, Bombay Beach, dead ahead. This felt like a hellish bombing run. Seventy-two degrees all of a sudden. Late afternoon and the sun was still high. The scream of a two-stroke engine got my eyes back on the road, some little jackass riding a four-wheeler over the rough gravel. He flipped me off and sped away. Guess I deserved that.

Bombay Beach probably used to be a cute little getaway cove. On a map it still looked like a retiree community, neat rows of small houses and double-wides within their chain-link fences. There were a few people trying to rally this place into a comfortable neighborhood while dealing with the remnants of a flood that wiped out a large portion of the waterfront homes. Whether it was defiance or just entropy, their response was to build a Great Wall of dirt between the town and the sea. One side of the dirt berm on Fifth Street was life in a micro-town, on the other the skeletal remains of a vacation cove, a reminder that they could be erased at any moment. The kid roared by on top of the dirt wall on his four-wheeler, another friend chasing close behind on a dirt bike.

I found an empty spot to park near Avenue E and Fifth Street, near a dirt ramp that led over the berm and out to the beach, such as it was. It was definitely colder out here. I reached back into the car for a scarf, then walked up to the top of the dirt ridge to survey the area. I had no idea if the houses nearby were occupied or squatted or abandoned. Some were more obvious than others, windows shattered and insides stacked with meth-chic furniture and garbage. There was life here, watching me from their caves. I was the outsider, the predator. They sensed it. Or maybe I was just psyching myself out.

I walked down the ridge to a house that looked like Godzilla sat on it. Paint flaked off waterlogged walls that bowed out. All the windows were gone. It was two stories, but only half of the second floor had a roof. The garage door was wrenched open at a diagonal, the bottom lip tagged in hot-pink paint marker, two-inch letters reading: SEE WHAT I SAW.

A filthy upturned sofa was the only thing keeping it open, fabric slashed, metallic ribs exposed, just another victim. Glass and plastic crunched underfoot with every step closer. The overwhelming smell of moldering foam and rotten wood oozed into my nostrils. I adjusted my scarf to cover my mouth. I knew enough about this place. I crouched, every sense tingling, hyperaware of my surroundings. I expected to see a crowd of angry townsfolk every time I checked over my shoulder, asking me what the hell I thought I was doing. Nothing but seagulls and dirt back there. I squinted inside. On the far wall, in neon paint marker in foot-high letters near the ceiling, the phrase SORRY DAD.

I poked my head under the garage door, impressed by some of the murals. The wall on the left was covered by a huge papier-mache poster of an old-timey Air Force pinup, dressed sharply in a radio operator's uniform. Her hair was perfect, sharp hat angled just-so on her head. Delicate fingers touched one side of her headset, pinky upturned. She was loving her work. A big speech bubble above her read YOU WILL HEAR THEIR VOICES WHEN YOU TRY TO SLEEP.

Her lower face was flaking and separating from the wall. When the wind spun through the garage, her chin flapped up to reveal a horrible skeletal smile painted beneath. Under other circumstances, I'd commend the artist for their sense of morbid playfulness. It settled back down as the wind died, and the woman's expression changed, her eyes a little colder, her stare a little more vacant.

Tricks of the light.

My fingertips vibrated. My ears buzzed. It was colder now than when I first arrived, and I couldn't stop sweating. I pulled the beanie off my head and jammed it in my waistband. Was this what it looked like when she'd been here? Was I seeing what she saw? That phrase, *you will hear their voices . . .* that was in Dee's journal.

I didn't want to venture any further inside. If Dee was out here, I didn't think she'd be in this place. I backed out under the garage door in a crouch, turning to come face-to-face with a skinny, leathery old woman. I shrieked, skittering backward and banging my head on the door, one hand clutching my burning scalp while the other instinctively drifted to my pocket to grab my knife.

"It's private property," she croaked. She wore a faded pink tank top, yellow cowboy boots, blue jogging shorts. Her hair was pulled back into twin pigtails, skin rough and pebbled like weathered cowhide.

"Sorry."

"It's not *my* private property." She smiled. "Did you take a picture?"

"Of what?"

She jutted her chin at the collapsing house.

"Not . . . no."

"You should. Won't be here forever. Could come in handy later. Video. Pictures. Sometimes that's all you get."

She dug into a small bag hanging from her neck and pulled out a small Ziploc bag with a neatly-cut white bread sandwich inside. "PB and J."

"I'm good."

"I seen enough tweakers come through here to know when someone's near collapse. I ain't judging you. Just saying, you look like you're about to drop. You might not see it, but I do."

I grabbed the sandwich, staring at the plastic. Who takes random sandwiches from a strange lady? I was hungry. I put it in my pocket and hoped she'd forget about it.

"You're not from around here. That radio around your neck means you're just like all the others that come waiting for the sky to open. You dropped a bunch of acid or meth or something because you thought it would make it easier to see the crack in the sky."

"I'm not on drugs. Not meth, anyway."

"It does help."

"What do you know about it? The uh . . . the thing everyone's out here looking for?"

"Well, I used to try to tell people all about it. I know things that nobody else does." Her eyes went wide as she said it, trying to drill the importance of a secret into me. She squinted at the phone in my hand. "Are you recording this?"

"No."

"Why not?"

"I didn't think—"

She tilted her head, that look of half bemusement, half disappointment only a mom could make. She ran her fingers through her hair and pulled her pigtails tight behind her ears, clearing her throat. She nodded at me. I stared at her until I finally grasped that she really was waiting for me to record her. I held the phone up and nodded, trying to humor her. I was conserving battery at this point. No way I was going to—

"Well?" she asked.

"Okay. All right, hold on . . . "

My thumb clumsily swiped over the camera button, bringing her feet into frame. There was a shadow over her legs, coming from the wrong direction, as if someone was standing next to her. I looked up from the phone, but the shadow wasn't there. Onscreen, a smudge on the lens next to her in the frame, just above her shoulder. I looked up again. Nothing.

"Hold on." I wiped the lens on my T-shirt, taking a step back and framing her again. Still that thin smear of fog above her shoulder. I wiped the screen down as well. "I think there's something wrong with—"

"Just press record, hon, the sky's gonna open up soon."

I didn't know if she meant the weather or the mysterious crack in everything.

She cleared her throat again. "This area used to be a military testing ground. Not a lot of people talk about that." She made a grand gesture, presenting the wall of dirt behind her.

"Have you seen two women pass through here?"

"Secret things. They was trying to make a bomb that would blow the Reds to a different place. Not blow them to Hell, just sort of . . . you know in the old cartoons when Bugs Bunny would be sweeping the floor, and instead of sweeping up the dust, he'd reach down and lift up the whole cartoon frame and sweep the dust under it? Like that. They were just gonna push 'em somewhere else. That was the idea. And they made a mistake. Or maybe everything worked the way it was supposed to. They rang existence like a bell."

"I'm just trying to find my sister."

"It's still echoing. It made a crack in everything. You can see it in the sky, but only from the Sea. Something's trying to come through. Or we're leaking out."

"Anyone else out here looking for it today?"

She shrugged. "I'm the lighthouse, guiding ships in. Just an antenna, you see. The signals are everywhere. I'm attuned. I know when people are ready for it, I just give them a nudge in the right direction."

Her eyes were wet and shiny, and she looked at me as if seeing me for the first time. "You have her eyes, you know?"

"Whose . . . "

"Your sister . . . you have her eyes . . . they got closer than anyone ever has. She was here. She just passed . . . "

"You've seen her?" I lowered the camera to look her in the eye.

She tipped her chin up a couple of times, indicating that I needed to raise the camera. I framed her face and it changed just a little onscreen. The fog-smear rippled up her shoulder and obscured her head. There was another face, just for a fleeting second, a wide mouth and eyes that were sunken and deep crimson. Not like a demon, like someone who'd had their eye sockets emptied. The shape cascaded off of her like water, rushing down to the ground and over the sand wall.

"Sometimes it's better if you don't get answers. It'll pull that pit out of your stomach, spit it right in your lap. Tie it on you like a necklace you can't break. You'll have the rest of your life to deal with that." She ran a finger across the small transistor radio tied to the lanyard on my neck. "Set your frequency. Radios work on two parts. The signal and the antenna. Keep recording. Even when you want to turn away. Is that phone case waterproof?"

I nodded.

"Good. You go over the dirt wall and you'll see a couple

of old posts sticking out of the sand. One of them has the guts of an old baby grand piano leaning up on it. Sit there. Get your radio on, 'cause them wires can really amplify the signals. Sit down for a minute and point the camera out there over the water. Point it to the North Shore. You'll get your answers."

She started climbing up the large dirt wall, stopping at the top, between me and the sun. Ten feet over my head, a perfect silhouette with a blazing halo. There were lines in the sky haloing her head. Purples and blues, spreading cracks like a bullet hole in glass. She kept walking. I followed her. She disappeared over the edge of the wall just as I crested it. I stood on top of the berm, the Salton Sea spread wide before me. There was nobody on the other side.

I'd never felt more alone than in that moment, standing on that dirt hill. I understood how big the world was and how small I was and how I'd never see Sharon again. There was a tiny pebble near my foot, so small compared to this hill, and me, just a pebble compared to the Sea.

Six seagulls flew over the water in an impossibly perfect circle, angled slightly as they dipped down to feed before ascending, a Ferris wheel askew.

Old, rusting hunks of trailers stood amidst the remains of a few wooden beach shacks, and there was a post, just like she said, the remains of a piano leaning against it. The wooden lid lay on the ground, almost polished, the gold Wurlitzer mark shining through caked mud. I stepped around white and black enamel-coated shards like the broken teeth of a mythical creature who had lost its final battle. It was the metal guts, whatever you call that part of a piano, leaned against the post, strings humming softly as the breeze blew across them.

Nobody here but me and the seagulls.

See what I saw, Sharon told me.

Look through the camera, the old lady said. So I did.

The wind kicked up, buzzing across the piano strings, and I heard them whisper. Faint, distant military call signs. Echo. Bravo. I felt sleep crawling over me, despite being on this stinking shore, growing colder. I'd pushed myself too hard. Maybe if I ate something. I reached into my pocket for that sandwich, but there was nothing there. Of course there was nothing there.

I opened up the video I'd just shot to watch the old woman again. It was ten minutes of me recording a dirt pile, punctuated by my answers to her questions.

The smear was still there. I watched, waiting for it to move, and just like before, it did. Pouring down, rippling over the wall, and a few moments later I felt a cold, wet static blast around my legs and thighs, heading out to the water.

I looked at the horizon to steady my eyes. Out on the lake, the birds dove, smacking down into the surface near a bag of trash, billowy white and drifting in the shallows, not too far away. I heard wind humming through the birds' feathers as they came down. They exploded into the water and came up swimming, some of them gulping fish, some just spinning in slow, confused circles. It was such a mesmerizing pattern, such a graceful dance, that I started recording them.

Above the phone, everything I saw was dull desert colors, dirt, slate water, grey clouds. On screen, the birds left faint ripple-traces of rainbow waves in their wake. Water exploded up from their impact, spraying diamonds and sapphires into the air. The trash bag morphed and grew, undulating on the water like a great reptile. One of the birds approached and gave it a poke, and it thrashed in response.

It was a person, floating face down. Their hand slapped the water twice, spine spasming. Were they swimming or drowning?

Offscreen, it was just dumb birds and garbage, quiet aside from the occasional ripple of water and wings. Onscreen, the person flailed wildly. I kept filming and waded out, approaching cautiously. It was a bunch of plastic. Two trashbags tied up inside a drop cloth. The water was up to my knees by the time I was next to it. The birds swam away, eyeing me cautiously.

I raised the phone up to frame a body. A woman, emaciated, wearing only a thin white dress, soaked through and translucent. On her right shoulder blade was an intricate tattoo that I'd seen before, a velociraptor skull painted with tribal designs above an old-school banner reading CLEVER GIRL.

I seized her by the shoulder and pulled. When my hand made contact, the world shook around me, like I'd been dropped from a great height into the deep end of a pool. It slapped me. There was no plastic in my hand. It was cold skin, bony arms.

"Dee? Dee, are you okay? Jesus Christ . . . "

I looked over the phone and she wasn't there. She was in my hand, I felt it, and she was there onscreen, facing away from me, staggering to her feet, water pouring off her head and from her mouth. She reached an arm out for support and turned to me with empty, blackened eye sockets.

I screamed.

Her skin was translucent, pale avocado. She shivered, her lips thin, purple, stretched over a smile like old tombstones. Her eyes were gone, sockets packed with silt from the lake bottom, leaking great muddy tears down her face. One socket was narrow and puckered, as if the eye had been gouged out. The other was blown wide, giving her a gruesome quizzical stare. She lifted her hands, mouthing a name.

"I'm not . . . I'm not here. You're not here," I said it over and over, checking offscreen to confirm it. Nothing in this lake but me, birds, and too many dead fish. Nobody around to see this, and I couldn't tell if that was for the best. Birds and mud and . . . in front of me, where the Dee onscreen should be standing, two perfect concentric circles, about the size of skinny legs. The water was bending around something.

I lifted the camera up to see her pathetic face, reached an arm out to the air to draw her close. I hated her so much, hated myself even more for trying to give her comfort. My arm passed through something that felt like TV static, dull electricity and cold, wet hair. I lowered the phone, fingers shaking, clutching it tight. My legs were numb. I slogged back to the shoreline, stopping every few feet to look back. I held the phone up and she was gone.

I slumped across the mud to the piano-post, lowering myself down carefully and leaning back against it to stare at the Sea. The sky pulsated, grey to deep blue to purple and back to grey, so slow I was convinced my eyes were playing tricks on me, dilating from the trucker speed or exhaustion.

The sand between me and the water's edge was like a great brush stroke, wide and spattered, tapering down to a thin line leading back to me. I started having thoughts about what to do for hypothermia, forgetting that I had a vehicle on the other side of this dirt wall with a heater. Next to my splatter-path was a series of slender footprints. A woman's bare feet. Keeping pace with me. Leading straight back to me. Standing next to me.

A perfect set of imprints, narrow heel, the curve of the arch, ten toes, nothing there to cause it. I checked to make sure I still had my boots on. The footprints were getting darker, as if something was still dripping off from being soaked in the sea, pressing down into the dirt.

I clutched the phone with shaking hands, focused on the footprints. Onscreen, two feet, pointing away from me. Pale avocado green. Emaciated calves, and a mass of wet, tangled black hair hanging down to obscure the rest of the screen until Dee snapped her head around to gaze at the camera.

I dropped the phone.

Laughter echoed around me, coming from the transistor radio on the lanyard around my neck. I brought it close to my ear and pushed at the volume wheel until the red light came on. The laughter stopped. I turned the radio off and the laughter broke in again.

"You're on the right station," the radio said.

I started to hold the phone up.

"Don't do it if you're scared to see me. I think I'm beautiful," Radio-Dee said.

"What happened? What happened to you?"

"Do you love Sharon?"

"You took her away. I came out here to . . . stop you."

"Kill me?"

"How's that for love?"

A long pause, then a new set of wet footprints appeared, then another. She was shuffling away from me.

"You might be too late. I'm not sure," her voice buzzed from the radio down into my chest. "Look at me. Please."

I aimed the phone at the newest wet footprints. Her feet appeared onscreen. I panned up to her face. She hid her eyes behind one hand.

"Is this easier?"

I nodded.

"When was the last time you talked to Sharon?"

"It was . . . Christmas? I think."

"Christmas of what year?"

"The year before you took her out here the first time, I guess."

She dropped her hands suddenly, exposing her empty eye sockets. Salty tears gushed in filthy rivulets of mud and blood. "Sorry, my arm was getting tired. Can I sit next to you?"

Before I could answer, a large wet spot formed in the dirt next to me, thighs and crisscrossed legs. A wave of static rushed over my left thigh.

"Please don't touch me."

The static receded.

Dee pointed out to the water. "I brought her where she wanted to go. I gave her everything she asked for."

"You took her away from her family."

"What family?" she asked. "You? You were the only one who'd talk to her, and that was what, a little check-in every month or so? Maybe an extra call if it was a birthday? And how often were you visiting her in the hospital?"

"Every day that I could."

"I checked those records. Once every three months at first? And then once or twice a year?"

"People have lives and jobs, shit to do and bills to pay. I'm a fucking grownup. You want me to apologize for living in a city that's grinding me to dust? I give everything I can *when* I can. And excuse the fuck out of me, but I've got one of those phones that also *receives* calls. Before all of this bullshit, how often did she call to see how I was doing? I'm her family. She's my family. That's all we had was each other. We got each other through the shit. When was the last time she reached out to me?"

"Four nights ago, in your dreams . . . "

"That's lovely, isn't it?"

I lowered the phone and looked around, thankful for once that nobody was here to see this. "I'm out here in the middle of the goddamned desert in the half-dark sitting and talking to myself, talking to a . . . to a puddle and a radio. When did I lose her?"

"I know how you feel. I do."

"She's my sister, you couldn't—"

"She was my wife."

"We used to talk. We used to talk all the time. When

we were kids. There was nothing I knew that she didn't. Nothing I wouldn't share with her."

I looked at my feet and picked at my shoelaces until they came untied, absentmindedly wrapping and unwrapping one around my index finger.

"I could see she was going through some shit. This was before she met you," I said. "I just wanted her to let me in. We'd already been through . . . well, a lot. A lot. And then suddenly, she became a fortress. Nothing in or out. The harder I pushed, the more closed off she got."

I looked at onscreen-Dee. She was sitting a lot closer than I'd thought, or maybe the camera made her *there* when my eyes told me otherwise. She had her knees drawn up, hugging them with one arm while she used the pinky on her free hand to dig into her eye sockets to pick out the muck.

"Does . . . that hurt?"

"It did. That one especially." She pointed at the larger hole on her face. "I deserved it. Sharon is . . . did she ever tell you about the night she tried to kill herself?"

"Which one?"

"There was more than one? That little bitch . . . " Dee rose from the sand and slapped at the dirt on her legs. I felt it spatter against me, an odd sensation coming from the open air. "You think you know someone . . . "

"She used to, when she would talk to me, she used to say how she just felt like she wasn't made for living in this world."

"I heard that one. She was in the wrong place, that everywhere was the wrong place."

"A half step behind everything and—"

"A little to the left," Dee finished the thought. "Heard that one a lot."

"I used to think it was about her coming out and how our family didn't accept it. I mean, that's a huge understatement. That was . . . I'd known she was gay since she was seven years old. She wasn't exactly public about it. But the first time I told her I knew without her telling me, she cried. She just hugged me, like . . . like trying to push herself through me, so tight. And then, somehow I was all she had. She wasn't good at making friends or talking to most people. She was convinced she was invisible, or just . . . I don't know, a sounding board. People loved to talk to her, or at her, but when she tried to share her thoughts, there was just a wall there, I guess. No one heard her, or at least that's what she'd say."

"Sounds like her."

"I just need to see her again, Dee. What did you do?" I pointed the camera at her face, looking over it at where I thought she was, my cheeks wet. "She's gone and I want to be invisible too."

"She never came back from this place. Things were rough for us before we came out here. She said she was done talking about it. That's the same thing she told me before she tried to . . . And then, just up the shore there, she took her tongue out. Cut it out. I had to visit her every day. I had to look at what I allowed to happen. That's how she wanted to tell me she was done talking. I had to carry that around for years. Figure out what I did to . . . but then I got it. She was done. And so am I."

We stared at the water. Small lapping waves that slowly erased the reflected clouds in the dying daylight. There was something else, just where the water got deep. Reeds. Grass, floating on the surface. Or was it hair?

"She never stopped loving you," Dee said. "That's why you're here, right? That's what you wanted to hear?"

The sky rippled like a giant flag, the air filling with a rush of static that started low and quiet, an intake of breath before some huge unknown creature bellowed its challenge. But it didn't stop inhaling. It rushed, climbing in pitch, and everything slowed down—the few birds left circling in the air bugged out for the shore.

71

I got up and stutter-stepped toward the sea, recording everything, the phone outstretched like a strange divining rod before me. The sky just . . . unraveled, a small tear somewhere near the horizon that flew over my head in a flash, some invisible scalpel zippering through the ether, drawing gouts of blue and purple light. I kept walking until my feet were wet.

When did I take my shoes off? I clutched the phone tighter.

It's waterproof, I whispered to nobody.

The fish carcasses and stones were sharp, but thankfully squished down into the mud before they could prick me too much. The water was freezing, but only at the surface. Below was warm, rushing static air. Above was desert chill. I kept walking, because Dee told me to on the radio.

I passed the floating trashbag again. And this time I saw it. Dee's body. The tattoo was visible under her dress. Tiny fish darted through her hair. Her arms were splayed, one hand weighed down by the small pistol curled around her finger.

I turned the camera toward the grass-hair-whatever on the water, praying I'd see her, but she wasn't there. Something was onscreen though, something I'd never be able to describe if given a thousand years. It wasn't a tentacle, not living, not leather or metal or full of bones or a blob, but it was there, thick as my leg, reaching up into the rip in the sky or reaching down from it. I couldn't tell.

When the water rose to my armpits, I lowered the phone and sank to my knees, crouching until my face went below. The world was murky and grey. Way out in the darkness, I saw more of that thing from the sky. A huge, slithering presence, golden and turquoise in the waves, a floating ball of formless snakes. I felt a shift in the center of my brain, something primordial, something a fish feels when a whale is charging, mouth open. It saw me. Inky stains spread in the water, emanating from the shape, coming closer. Tentacles, carrying her body. The water stung my eyes. My head pounded and I stood, sucking in great lungfuls of air, coughing.

"What is happening?" I asked. Then I screamed it. Screamed it at the horizon until I felt my throat crack. I turned to the shore to scream it back to the world. Someone had to answer for this. The answers I was getting, were as damning as the old lady said they'd be. Dee had told the truth in that journal. There was a crack in the sky, and it carried me on a tide through time, backward and forward simultaneously. I saw Dee in two states, her lifeless corpse nearby, her talkative spirit very present in the whatever-this-is.

"A crack in everything," I whispered.

My words echoed back from the sky, amplified, harmonized. They stretched into an endless choral chant that sounded like one long note, soft, soothing, familiar. My name.

Zula.

Zuuuula.

Zula, Zula . . .

Behind me, a splash, followed by a primal howl. I tried to turn, but something slammed into me, wrapping arms around me, tipping me off balance and into the water. I pushed away, disoriented, scrambling to my feet. I stood up, clearing water from my eyes.

Sharon.

Much thinner, her arms hard-muscled, veins raised above purpled skin. She wore a black version of Dee's simple dress. She smiled, eyes so warm, full of tears, open mouth displaying that horrible mangled lump of tongue. She howled again, and again, a longer keening that turned into full-on crying as she clutched me close. Her arm slid around my neck to comfort me. Her mouth moved, breathing a wordless song into my skin. Far away, drifting on the wind, it came to me, staticky, distorted, through the speaker on my transistor radio.

It was the song she made up for me as kids. She sang it to me every night after we were tucked into bed, and as we grew, it became sparser. She'd only sing it to me if we'd been apart for a while, just a few bars as a secret greeting.

"I love Zula, she is my stars and moon . . . "

I slumped down into the water, clutching at her leg.

"Everything's broken."

She nodded.

"There's a crack in the sky."

She started crying.

"You're my only family and you're gone. She took you away. It was already too late before I started."

"No such thing as too late," the radio around my neck said. "You found me. I reached out and you found me. You always can."

"I'm sorry." I whispered it again and again, watching the sky pulse, everything going purple and white, brighter and softer, slowly fading.

"I just wanted to tell you—"

"Zula," she sang again, moving away from me. I filmed her on the phone as she danced away across the surface of the water. My last family. My last friend. My last connection to the world, gone four years, and gone again and gone a third time.

I turned the phone to my face and said goodbye, said I'm done, said *It's waterproof* because it wouldn't matter. There would never be evidence beyond the bodies they find here. My sister's life was one of love and adventure. Dee did this, and left me to pick up the pieces. And I won't. I'm done.

"Don't follow me, Zula," she said. "You are my moon . . . "

I sank to my knees and turned onto my back, floating in the sea, watching the crack in the sky stop bleeding. It knit itself up and the clouds dissipated, wild constellations dancing over my head. The water was warm, so warm it matched me and I couldn't tell where I stopped and it began. I was the sea, reflecting the sky and the universe and my sister was gone. I wanted this to last as long as possible.

I was . . . I am her moon and her stars and her everything.

April, α – April, Ω

Look at you on that bed. I can't look at you on that bed. You hate me now, your silence speaks that forever. Remember when we were in love. That's not a question. That's what I tell you every

day, the first thing I say when I sit on your bed. You lock eyes with me and you stare through me and all I see is anger there, all I see is the emptiness in your mouth

and I know somehow that's my fault. But I stare at you until your chest hits a more regular rhythm, when I see the resignation set in that I'm not leaving, when I see

you accept that yet again, you can't call the nurse to make me leave because you're catatonic, or at least you pretend to be to them. I tell you, remember when we were in love. Remember when I loved you.

Remember when I bumped into you on the corner of Santa Monica and Hancock and I almost knocked you on your ass.

I was drunk. You were happy. We were both happy by the end of the day. You were out and you dragged me out and then we were out but I was too careful. And you tried. You tried for years and now I'm trying, because none of this should have happened.

Remember.

I see your face at night. When I close my eyes to sleep your face floats inches above mine, pale and angry and you're not screaming, just gritting your teeth, and your eyes are so

wide they're glowing, and you open your mouth and you're singing, but there's no sound, just starlight, endless universe pouring out of your mouth and rushing around me and lifting me and pulling me. And that's why you're angry, I see

it now. I'm writing it on the edges, because he was right, whoever wrote in this journal

before us, they were right, and they were waiting for us. I think you got connected to something that wasn't meant scared then and I'm scared now. And I'm tired of living scared. I wanted to tell my mom about

for you, but somehow is still right for us, and I am scared. I was scared then, in West Hollywood, surrounded by nothing but peace and love and everyone supporting us, I was

this. She's shaky on everything lately. I think she's using again, or close to it. She asks about you all the time, even when I ask her not to, because it hurts. She tells me it should hurt, and that if it

doesn't hurt, then it didn't mean anything. She says to revel in the hurt. I'm trying

to move into it or past it or something, I don't know. Artists, right? I bet she'd tell me to follow this through. Or not, who knows?

Remember that I love you. It's a mantra for me at night, when the

shadows come. When I

don't see your face, dark rooms split open, the silence fills with static screams. As it did that night at the sea. I think about what you told me, that I had to give up something to see it or hear it. I think that it's punishing me, sometimes, whatever it is. When it's quiet at night, or should be quiet, I hear the slightest rush of radio static. In the dark I see sparks of color. Blacks are never steady, they swim, they pour, shadows slide and wobble at the edges. If I'm alone and the windows are open at night, I smell salt water and dead fish. My skin is the only reliable thing, this soft vessel that's my only protection against everything, but it feels like I'm some kind of single-celled thing swimming in an ocean I don't understand. Sometimes if I look at my arms in dim light, I see things beneath my skin, moving, crawling like lines of ants. So, I spend my nights trying to remember. That's the only thing that pushes back against those sounds, those feelings and smells and sights. But is it pushing back? Or does my connection to you, my yearning to reconnect, does that calm them, it, whatever it is?

All I do is remember. All I do is think that maybe you were right. Because the world doesn't feel worth anything

with you here and
me somewhere else.
You went through a
door that we weren't
supposed to cross,
but I think you want
me there with you,
and that's a chance
I'm willing to
take. We're
going to go
back there
and find that
moment.
We're going to
remember
that
connection, or
reconnection,
or ignition, or
explosion, we're going to live in that
forever. And if anyone is looking for us,
they can follow this map, and if
they're brave enough to cross over, let
them come.

III.

START AGAIN

2018-Echo-2015-Echo-2018

Jeremiah 9:1

SHE'S DEAD and she's not. As a parent, is there new grief after this? First tooth. First day at school. They make friends, they leave for college. All of these things, even the happy ones, bring their own special sadness. That little piece of them that was just for you is suddenly bigger, shared, different. Death makes you understand, *really* comprehend what loss is. Grieving ebbs and flows, but the string, the raw nerve that gets cut when the body that was in your body disappears, you feel it in different degrees depending on the day. Depending on the weather. The wind. A song on the radio. A building. A body of water.

Her memory echoes like a scream in my skull. Everywhere I look reminds me of something. The sky reminds me of where she broke and how she died. Paper. Paint. Ink. A pen. A goddamned pen reminds me of her last days. I'm an artist. *Was* an artist. What can I create with now? Why would I bother? I haven't even been able to drink a glass of water since they found her in the sea. Can you imagine? The day I learned she was truly gone, I thought, *she was the best thing I ever created, what's the point of anything after this?* And that's selfish and stupid to say, because *she* was her greatest creation. I was just there to support.

I try to let her go, but she won't stop talking to me. Memories find their level. You try to hold them down and they just bubble up somewhere else. It's not in your control. None of this was in my control.

I tried to paint. Sketch. Write. All of it was about her. And none of it felt right, because it was just me trying to bring her back, or trying to make a physical embodiment of the pain I was feeling. I had a stack, this massive stack of blank canvases, and I just told myself every day: paint one line. Make one thing. It didn't work. I turned into such a cliché, found a razor and started hacking those canvases apart, because even that, those blank spaces with a single line, it was like trying to draw a map back to her. Then I looked at my arm, clutching the blade, and I thought *just one line*. One straight line. Down the road, not across the street.

I painted all of those canvases red. Stumbled out of my house, and because history is a wheel, was found cold and pale, near dead in the middle of the street just like her. Somebody called the cops as I lay bleeding but never checked up on me. That's L.A. Like I was just inconveniencing the cul-de-sac on my way out. That was two years ago, and obviously I recovered somewhat. Became an emptier version of me, but in starting to learn to live with myself I started learning to live without her.

I got a tattoo, which I swore I'd never do, in simple courier font on the inside of my left forearm: <u>Start Again</u>. Five inches long, starting in the middle of my softest skin, forever underlined in angry pink that just won't fade. Some hipster girls at my local coffee shop saw it once and asked me which studio did the scarring, said it was so *rad*. Maybe not rad. I don't know what words the kids use now and I don't give a shit.

In the past, when I'd fail, or lose a sale, get a review that said my work was shit, or reductive, or derivative, or any of the thousand, thousand little humiliations artists have to go through, I'd always say it to myself after a good bout of wine and crying: Start again. I don't know why I got the tattoo. Who did I have now that loved me or that I loved?

I used to . . . When it got too quiet in the house, once I was alone, truly alone, sick of music, sick of podcasts, I'd dig out any old recordings I could find of Dee. Band recitals. School theater. Old answering machine tapes. I just needed to hear her. Having her in the air in the house stopped the roof from collapsing. And I thought . . . maybe exploring that would be my way back. Maybe hearing her again would be like holding her hand as she led me somewhere safer.

One of my favorite podcasts was *The Memory Show*, everyone's favorite found-audio showcase, hosted by Kfira Gardner. That's how I met Campbell Parker. She was Kfira's other half, the host of her own show, and I guess if they find this recording, maybe this will be the last episode. Campbell would tell you herself, but she's . . . not entirely here. I see her over there in the corner. Her arms are at a weird angle. So is her head, I guess. Her mouth is bub-bub-bubbing up and down, and every time her chest raises I hear a rush of radio static. Maybe she's in there, maybe there's still hope. I don't know. I don't think anyone will find us in time. I've lost a lot of blood. Again.

The intro! Do the intro.

Every episode of *The Memory Show* started with Kfira saying *everything in the world is a personal recording device*. Think of a tree in a park. Is it just a plant? Is it the spot where someone fell in love? Two notes on a guitar take you back to high school, on the hood of your car, feeling summer air on your skin and watching your friends swim in a lake. A lake can . . . uh . . . Everything is a recording device, and time is a map we can only see once we've arrived, the path marked by little victories and sadnesses, joy and tragedies. And . . . I don't remember all of it.

I loved that show. Was so excited to be part of it. That Dee could be . . . But that's not what this is. *The Memory Show* belonged to Kfira Gardner. This, I guess, is the final episode of *Salton Signal*, with your host Campbell Parker. Exploring the mysteries and rumors that surround the Salton Sea. If you're hearing this, or I guess if you've heard any episode of the show, you know who I am. Today, you get to hear everything about me. Everything about me, and my little Dee-Bee.

. . . Did you hear that? Did you hear her? Just now?

All of this is . . . my brain has gone bad. I'm not remembering any of it. Memory is . . . Before I found success as an artist, I spent ten years in a job I hated, and I could barely tell you a thing about a single minute from that office. I remember the day they hired me, and I remember not getting a cake or a card the day I left. But ask me about the day someone told me they'd pay me money to make art. Ask me about the day Dee was born. Ask me where I was driving the first time I heard her sing from her car seat. How filled with joy I was when she graduated high school. How proud and scared I was when she came out to me. Ask me about the day the police called to tell me she'd been found in the desert with Sharon. Ask me about the day my husband blamed me for what happened to her. We were already apart by that time, but the way he said my name and her name . . . and that was when she was still alive. Ask me about Sharon's sister Susan finding Dee at the Salton Sea. Dead. Ask me to draw a map of my life, that's the constellation you'll see. Joy to pain to joy and on to pain and pain and pain.

It's hard enough to walk through life, but when you carry pain and loss? If you're out doing things it's easy to kind of keep that balloon floating behind you, right? But it's always tied to your belt. And then you get home and eventually you have to stop moving, and it floats over your shoulder, sometimes just outside of your peripheral vision. How can you run from something when your shoes are made from it, when it's woven into your clothes, grown into your skin? Loss doesn't follow you, it lives with you, like a roommate you don't see for a few days at a time, waiting to pop out at the strangest times.

I didn't think I'd ever be ready to talk about this. I still haven't processed it. It's been years. They never found Sharon's body, but they ruled out foul play. The day they made that official was the day I slid back into using. And now, I feel like . . . besides whatever blood I have left keeping me breathing, Dee's spirit is the last thing in my body. I'm almost empty and it's all pouring out. Committed beyond commitment.

I never even tried to start dealing with any of it. Even alone, I couldn't speak it into the air. All I hear from Dee now, the way she's there on the water, in the corner, in my chair, down the hall, always *there* and always silent. Silence can be deafening. The loudest noise, right? If you hear pure silence, you can't hear anything else, and today, I really tried for that purity. I don't know where Dee is, and I know exactly where she is—right in front of me, but not there, in my mind, always in my mind.

I left my house with Campbell Parker a few days ago to . . . I wonder if anyone's filed a report yet? Shit. I left my house a few days ago because I swear . . . this sounds crazy, I swear, Dee came back.

She found me. I found her. But there was a wall between us. A misunderstanding. I'm going to tell you about all of this, and I'm going to reference some things. They're all here in my notes, which I'm sliding into my backpack. It's a red . . . shit, I don't know the brand name. Red backpack with a purple ribbon tied around one of the zippers. It has my name on the inside, Aisling. I know, crazy spelling, hippie parents. That's why I went by AshLynn in college, a-s-h-l-y-n-n, because I thought it looked cooler, I guess. It also says #reSISTER in sharpie across the back, because . . . well, I guess I'm one of *those* SoCal women. I'm just putting this on the record in case you, listener, find my body and there's no backpack. Or if you find this recorder in a backpack and there's no body. I was here and this all happened. You have me from now until the batteries run out of juice, or I do.

Nobody else was supposed to get hurt.

Salton Signal listeners, my daughter's name is Dee Bolan. She kept my maiden name. I was eighteen when I had her and our family, when it was whole, which wasn't that long, I guess, we weren't big on tradition and patriarchy and . . . well, anyway. My name is Aisling Esperanza, yes, *that* one with the famous performance art piece in the subway, *The Hallway Eternal. The Reunion* piece I did with that egotistical gasbag of an ex. People ate that one up, too. Anyway.

Ash, I always tell people, call me Ash. Esperanza, Ashes and Hope . . . I suppose you know our story, sort of, from this show or dozens of others that have picked apart my family's life, like *Cracked Skies,* or *Slab City Skies* or *Rhapsody in Dee*—Goddammit who thought that was a good name for a show? My daughter was exploring the Salton Sea with her wife, Sharon. Something happened. You know all this, right? Of course you do. If not, go download one of those shows—not the *Rhapsody* one, fuck you Pamela Baker—they'll fill you in. You can come back to this and we'll be all caught up.

Just in case maybe you're a police officer standing over one to three dead bodies, wondering what happened, I guess I should say I'm here in the desert because years ago, the police called to tell me my daughter had been found frozen half to death in the middle of a dark highway. And she kept getting pulled back here, all because of a legend about a cracked sky.

When she told me about it, I told her I believed her. I believed she saw what she thinks she saw. Which sounds like I don't believe her, I know. I didn't say that part out loud. I wanted her to feel loved and secure and trusted, and she was right. I see it too. It's right outside the window. It's in the hole in the wall. It's pouring through the broken glass. The light is on, and the moths are bashing against the windows, trying to break through. Dee saw Sharon open that door, and then later she went through it, and that door opened another door where Sharon was gone. That door, someone needs to oil the damn thing. The hinges are rusted and screaming.

I know, I'm being maudlin. This is the last thing I get to tell anyone, at least give me this. This is my last . . . I don't know what this is. Last will and . . . who am I leaving behind? I'm recording this for posterity, or an explanation, or . . . a record. A sign that I was here, that this really happened. If my voice—am I talking too loud? You know what's funny is how Kfira Gardner always ended every show by saying *every memory is a recording, find a way to hold on to it!* That's all that's left of me now. I mean . . . will be. There's nobody left out there who loves me or knows me and this was just stupid, stupid . . . Campbell didn't have to try to find me out here. This didn't have to involve anyone else.

And if it sounds like I'm rambling to avoid my feelings, well . . . yeah. Starting means I'm that much closer to the end, and maybe I'm not as ready as I thought I was. The picture will come out, like a Pollock. That's all this is. An explanation.

Reality has been a little inconsistent for me these past few days, but these are the constants: My daughter is dead.

Her partner . . . wife . . . Sharon, is dead. That's in the past, and it hasn't changed. Your host, Campbell Parker . . . this is probably her last episode. My name is Ash. There's another woman here, Doreen, I left her upstairs. I always thought if we met I'd strangle her. She helped me see things, and she found everything she'd always been looking for. Her eyes are wide open now.

Do you hear Campbell? Can you? She hasn't stopped moaning, but all I hear is a weird static blast in the air. What does that sound like on the recording? She's there and not there, crying out, and I can't hear a sound over my own heartbeat, over Dee's constant whispering.

What a finale, right?

Sorry, I was planting signposts. Reliable truths: Remember Dee. Remember Ash, her mother. Come back to that, even if nothing else makes sense. Hold those constants, because they won't change even as the world changes around us. At the end of this, I don't know if everything will be as I'm saying it, but I do hope this survives. This recording, or a transcript of it. It might not be the way anyone remembers it happening, but this is how it happened to me.

I want to show you how the Sea is a whirlpool, pulling everything in. The Sea was, briefly, a place of hope. They called it the Salton Riviera, a miracle in the desert, and then it was gone, just as ephemeral and wavering as any other memory. I didn't know what that word meant, do you? *Ephemeral*. That means here for a short time, basically. I remember my grandpa used to say that when he'd come to visit. "I ain't here for a long time, I'm here for a good time." Words to live by.

But watch that whirlpool. The first time Dee came back from the sea, she kept a journal. Just like the notebook she found out there, full of scribbled, pained writing and drawings of whirlpools, big black spirals. Maybe something wrote through her. Dee pulled Sharon into this, or was it the other way around? I'm doing this from memory with no way to remember what I already talked about, so sorry if we drift around. I just . . . can finally, *finally* get all of this off my chest. There is no such thing as a reliable memory. Ephemeral. Isn't everything, on a long enough timeline?

I have spent years putting Dee away. Or just . . . dealing with . . . you know, every time I say it, I know it doesn't sound true. I was trying to get to a place where I could wake up in the morning and live my life, and maybe, if I thought of her, it would be something happy and I'd smile. But that never happened. I was listening to an old recording we made, back when she was a kid, me talking to her before a band recital. I can still see her crooked teeth and that dress that was tight in the wrong places and just made her look like an awkward green velvet pillow, but she felt pretty so I told her she was pretty, and she *was*! She was *so* pretty that night. She told me there was a girl she liked in the band, and I asked if they were friends, and she said she wanted to like her the way she sees people on TV like each other. That was her grasp of things. And that feeling, you see? That rush of love that comes in, when you remember, how it just . . . you start to feel bad but love burns all the negativity away. I wanted other people to feel that. I wanted to find a way to share that with the world. That's the start of how I ended up on *The Memory Show*.

My last attempt at . . . not performance art, but collective art, art as healing . . . I started a website where I invited people to share pieces of their lives, little audio and video snippets, and a few words explaining why the videos were so special to them. The only criteria was that it had to be someone you loved who had passed away. A digital garden of remembrances. I don't know that I believed in it, but I needed something to do. Keep my head above water. I had it designed so that you could choose to just read a memory, listen to a file, or watch a video, but it would reset if you switched away from the browser. You had to fully experience it. And maybe in that, we could find pieces of ourselves in others, and connect. You'd fill in their gaps and they'd fill in yours, and you'd just understand together that you could, if not move on, then at least keep moving.

It got a little bit of buzz, if for no other reason than people wanted to see a famous artist react to the death of their child, I guess. I didn't want publicity. I didn't even have my name attached to it, but people put two and two together. The internet is nosy. They started digging into any video that didn't have a lot of detail. Looking for connections to celebrity or scandal or . . . I don't know why the internet does what it does. Once the cat was out of the bag and people knew this was my project, I tried to lean into it.

I did some minor press but asked for privacy. The website got noticed by Kfira Gardner from *The Memory Show*. More accurately, it caught the eye of Campbell Parker, who was helping her friend produce the show. They were like Dee and Sharon. Together, I mean. A couple. I wonder if that's part of the whirlpool too, that they were in love, not married, but together for a while, Campbell and Kfira. Could you envision a more perfect NPR-sounding couple?

Campbell contacted me via my website about doing an interview for *The Memory Show,* and I said yes. A bigger audience for Dee, and maybe a chance to do a safe interview on NPR, a space where I could get it all out and then rightfully tell future inquiries that I said all I needed to say about everything.

Campbell sent me a little pre-Q&A for the interview. Basic questions about me, my art, studiously avoiding asking about Dee beyond the scope of the project. Some people would think she was showing respect, but it turned out to be the kind of respect you show a rabbit by putting a carrot near a snare. I didn't realize, didn't do my research, that Campbell Parker was the host of *Salton Signal*, and that of course she knew more than my name and my art. Neither of us realized that was the moment we'd strayed too close to shore, into ankle-deep waters, and the whirlpool had us.

I was scared about all of it, I'll admit. I got myself ready for the interview the only way I knew how at that point. Good ol' backsliding. Tomorrow's outfit would require long sleeves.

I woke up that morning, proud that I hadn't overdone anything. Like, I literally looked at my kit on the bedside table and thought, *that's how you do it*. I was alert. Good to drive. I showed up for the interview and met Campbell in the lobby of a classroom building on a college campus, because I guess that's how NPR stations work? I don't know. She looked like you'd imagine someone who helps her wife create a podcast about old cassette tapes would. Short hair, clippered on the sides and all slick and cool on top. Her eyes were watery and blue, and her teeth were a little too perfect. Really sharp jawline, like . . . like if a bird owned a hip coffee joint. One of those jawlines you could see even if she wasn't facing you. I couldn't tell how old she was. She had on this Led Zeppelin T-shirt, the one with the prism and the rainbow, is that . . . no, *Floyd*. Whatever. She had on a blazer and Doc Martens, like that was her uniform. I had a coat I loved like that once, too. So did Dee.

I still . . . I'm sorry to think this, or maybe I'm not, because I loved . . . *love* my daughter . . . when I see women, I will still instinctively think *she might play for Dee's team*. Part of my brain hasn't let go, and I will honestly think, *oh, she's not with Sharon anymore, maybe this one . . .* Androgynous? Genderqueer? I don't know, Dee would set me straight on that. She knew all the terms. Nobody really classified like that when I was . . . in the scene? God, I sound so out of touch. Wish I could edit this thing.

I used to love introducing women to her. She hated

93

that. I didn't *know* she hated it, thought I was being Cool Mom, you know, but she was really protective of . . . not her identity, her heart. I wish I had helped her with that, asked her more about it. I was an artist for Christ's sake, it's not like I hadn't seen same-sex couples, people actively exploring humanity with their bodies and hearts and minds. It took me a long time, well after she'd met Sharon, to really understand that she wasn't trying to hide being gay. She wasn't afraid of people knowing. There was something else with them. I wish I would have asked.

Campbell.

She introduced herself, and the way she said my name, I should have known something was up. I've met some huge fans in my time, and the excitement she showed was different. Didn't read right. She brought me down the hall to a little lounge, said we'd get started out here because some other host just finished recording in studio A and he was a heavy smoker with bad gas. She lit a spa candle in there and wanted to give it twenty minutes to cleanse. She introduced me to her assistant, or the show assistant, I can't remember now. She didn't follow us to the sea, and maybe if I don't record her name, and if she's smart enough to stay quiet, none of this will find her. Let's make up a fake persona. Her name was Hippie Girl. She had long, thick brown hair that just kind of went everywhere, and she wore this really soft-looking sweater, and she was just . . . like a hug in human form.

We went through a few pleasantries, where I carefully avoided talking about myself, or even really Dee. Campbell probed at the edges of the bigger story, *her* bigger story. When she asked me why I was doing this project, I said it's because I love my daughter and I'm terrified of forgetting her. Every day, something else slips away. And I try to hold on to all of it, because memory comes back hard sometimes, like a phantom punch to the stomach. I'm tired of picking myself up off the floor. I didn't say that, any of it. Just the part about loving her. How it would help to remember.

Then we went into the main studio, where Campbell introduced me to Kfira Gardner. She made all of these not-jokes about how it was a pure accident that she was wearing souvenir socks from my *Urban Valkyrie* piece, and coincidence that she had the coffee table book from the LACMA installation I did a decade ago, but if I wouldn't mind signing it on the way out . . .

I laughed the way I imagined she wanted. Touched her forearm in a way she'd relate in stories to friends. Made eye contact that bordered on flirty. All of that. Performing human.

She started the recording, keeping things conversational, asking a few extra questions here and there. We weren't live, so there were no worries about stutters or curse words. Kfira asked if I wanted to listen to some of Dee's recordings with her. We did, and it was fine, though I was surprisingly emotional hearing them in this context. Not *Hallmark-movie* emotional. Feral, protective, afraid. I wanted everyone to feel that love I felt. I worried Kfira would make a face, some small tic that would betray that she thought Dee was boring, that these recordings were worthless. But she didn't. She was impassive, a pro, though she did smile at this part where a younger Dee talked about wanting to play the chooba in a band. I tried to correct her, and she started making tuba noises and then fart noises, and I lost it, laughing.

I asked if they were putting all of that in the show, and she said they would. Snippets of Dee would be spread throughout a few episodes as they went over different aspects of family recordings, memories, all of that.

Pieces of my daughter. Happy little . . .

But I felt good afterwards. I felt good for the first time in a long time, even if this *good* was just really a variant of *not bad*.

When we came out of the studio, Campbell was there to greet me and offered to take me on a tour of the facilities. I said yes, because, you know, *feelin' good* and all of that. You do an interview and then people want to take you around to meet other people, or just be seen with you, or genuinely show you something they find interesting.

She took me to this listening room they had set up for *The Memory Show*, all of these huge stacks of records and boxes of cassettes and other things. Plastic milk crates labeled DONE and BROKEN and RESTORE. The room was maybe ten-by-ten feet. The walls were bare white cinderblock, with one big corkboard on the back wall covered in post-it notes, photos, and a big map of southern California. At the top of the board, in those multicolored plastic letters you find on refrigerators, it said WHERE THE MAGIC HAPPENS.

There was a small table in the middle of the room with a machine on it, three sets of headphones. I'd never seen anything like it, like a breadmaker turned on its side, and all over the table this colorful plastic, like really short loops of streamers curling into a colorful tumbleweed. Campbell said this was a Dictabelt machine. Do you know what those are?

Imagine these bright plastic strips, translucent purple and red and blue. Really pretty, they just scream 1960s to me. They were the hottest thing in technology for a while. The machines were a more efficient way to take dictation, hence the name. You get about fifteen minutes of audio. The little belts were so light and foldable, it became a great, cheap way to send audio around the country. Cheaper than reel-to-reels, more durable than vinyl. Revolutionary, and forgotten. That's the way the world works. You don't really make a mark if what you do doesn't break anything, if there's no explosion or damage, your revolution, your whole life just kind of fades away, scraped from history like dead skin.

The Dictabelt machine, how they work—sorry, I keep

veering off, but I swear this'll pay off in a second—leaves a groove pressed into the plastic, so it's like a combination record player and cassette thing. You put the Dictabelt in the machine on this plastic spinner, and the needle cuts a groove in the plastic, slowly moving down as the belt spins. One use only. Campbell said all of the belts in the room came from an airstream trailer in the desert. They guessed the recordings were somewhere between fifty and sixty years old. And Dee was on one of them.

Campbell didn't know this, not yet. Nobody did. She asked if I wanted to listen, and what with the nature of my art project, I said yes. We fired up the machine. I watched the plastic waving by in the little window. At first, all I heard was static and equipment noises, hisses and pops. Then, there was the unmistakable rattling noise of a microphone being positioned. That's what Campbell said was happening.

Then came footsteps. A deep voice spoke a first and last name, followed by a series of tones. Not a tune, just a vaguely electronic, random progression of varying length and pitch. After the beeps another person repeated the name and added demographic info. A man's voice would say "Charlene Fowler", and then a woman would repeat the name and say an address and phone number. Never the same man or woman twice. No indication if the woman on the tape was indeed Charlene Fowler or if she was reading from a list. Campbell said she thought it sounded like recordings of numbers stations. I didn't know what those were either, but I don't want to digress again, you can Google it.

Near the end of the recording, the man said, "Raymond Wood," and the name stretched and roared, like a jet engine taking off. Just higher and higher, exploding into a burst of static, and underneath that, a girl's voice, buried.

She said my name, my address, my phone number. She said *start again*. Then the recording stopped.

I looked at Campbell. She shrugged and started to turn the machine off, telling me about some other things we could listen to if I wanted. I didn't know what to say. I briefly forgot how to speak. I didn't want to sound crazy, so I tried to keep the question vague.

"Did you hear that part at the end? The voice, the girl's voice? The start—" I didn't want to reference my tattoo, didn't want to talk about that scar.

Campbell shook her head. I asked if she could rewind it and play it again.

She backed it up a bit, and the man on the recording said *Raymond Wood* again. The weird squelch. The audio ramping up into the stratosphere. My name, my phone number. *Start again.*

I stared, trying to pull a reaction out of her. Thirty seconds passed and I broke. "Well?"

"Well what?"

"The voice? After Raymond Wood? It's hard to make out under the noise that comes after the man's voice."

"Raymond who? What man?"

I told her to play it again, to listen under the static.

"There wasn't any static. There's nothing. It's just quiet. Oh, there was like, that, bump? At the end? Kind of sounded like he pushed away from the table and opened a window or something? I could hear maybe . . . birds singing?"

I didn't know what to say. I grabbed the controls and rewound it again, apologizing. I could tell by her face she was getting a little nervous. I told her I needed to hear it again, swore I heard something. I asked her to switch headphones. Maybe mine were on a different channel or something. She said that wasn't how this player worked, but she humored me.

Again. My name again, unmistakable. "There!" I shouted as she started to speak it.

"I don't . . . I'm sorry, I'm not hearing anything. It cuts

98

off after Preston . . . Markson? I couldn't make out the name. Then the table noise and the birds."

"But you heard everything else."

I'd left the Dictabelt playing. Campbell had been stopping it at the end every time, shutting it off right after the part with my name, whether she knew it or not. Forty seconds, maybe fifty seconds into the silence, Dee returned.

"Do you know where I am?"

I felt this . . . what I was saying about loss a second ago, I felt that inside, like my heart had been a closed door, and suddenly something kicked it open and all of this cold air poured into my chest. I started gasping. My eyes darted around the room, looking for anything to stabilize myself. I stood up, sat down, missed the chair and bumped onto the floor. I heard Campbell asking if I was okay. I looked at the corkboard, finally noticing the entirety of the map pinned there. It was the desert near Palm Springs, and the Salton Sea was on the right. From where I sat, I could probably hide the whole thing behind my thumb.

Maybe it was a trick of the light, but a jagged line raced across the map as my eyes filled with tears. The water on the map turned a deeper blue and started to ripple. I wasn't crying. The rest of the room was in focus, if that makes sense. The *map* was alive and rippling. There were clouds reflected in the surface of the water. I stood up and moved toward the wall. Touched the map. It felt like . . . well, it felt like paper. I don't know what I was expecting. The water kept moving though, and from this new angle, there was sand, rocks, a shoreline. Two small dots moving away from the Sea. Was it them? Was I floating above? Was I still in the room?

"Ash? Ms. Esperanza, are you okay?" Campbell's voice. I blinked and then the map was just a map.

"Yes. Yes, sorry. I was just . . . I guess I had a bit of a rough day last night. This is the anniversary of . . .

something bad. Bad day for me." It wasn't. I'm a terrible liar. "I just . . . . I think I need a nap. You really didn't hear anything?"

"Just birds."

I excused myself and went home, straight to bed, but not to sleep. I'd like to say I tossed my kit in the garbage, but I put it away a little too reverentially. Slid it into the drawer. Thought, *in case of emergency, break glass . . .*

I sat against the headboard, knees pulled in close, watching the phone, convinced it would ring, certain Dee would be calling any minute now. The red LED on the answering machine—yes, I still have one—was burning a hole in my retina. I haven't gotten a new message in years, probably. Nobody has my home line, but I have some voicemails from Dee that I can't bring myself to delete. I made recordings of them to keep them safe, but throwing the machine out would be like throwing her out. Turning off the phone would mean she wouldn't know how to call me. Does that make sense? Just knowing she's there, part of her, by my bed . . . that helps me sleep sometimes. Not today. I hit play. I had these messages memorized like a teenage anthem, one of those songs you'd know the words to forever. I knew every breath and rattle and hiss and . . . I still hoped she'd be there, really there, new and alive, somewhere around the edges.

Hey ma, got your message, we're coming over Saturday still, let me know if I should bring anything.

Beep.

Hey ma, it's me. Just wanted to see what's new and how you're doing. Sharon was going to come by tonight to check on you, see if you need anything.

Beep.

Hey ma . . .

I hit stop. I used to joke with her that I should legally change my name to some cool spelling of "Hey Ma". *Hejma. Aymuh.* She never thought it was as funny as I did.

I looked at the red digital six on the machine. Until today, this was the most recent thing I had of her as an adult. And now I knew she was somewhere else. Had been somewhere else. I looked up at the ceiling, saw the time was almost midnight. I have a clock that projects the time up there so I don't have to sit up to check, I don't want you to think I'm crazy. But that means the sun had set, because you can't see it during the . . . you get it. I hadn't slept. I wasn't going to sleep. I was watching the sheets, watching the walls, watching the air.

I did what I always do when the house felt empty or I'm lonely or scared. When it's too quiet, when my heart surprises me by breaking for the umpteenth time from a new variation on an old pain, I ask her questions. I don't know if I believe in an afterlife, but I believe in it when I talk to her. I never ask about what happened. New questions would linger unanswered, I know that. New questions would remind me of how I failed. How she's gone. Outliving a child brings another curse beyond eternally missing them: all the things you did wrong, all the choices you could have changed. You spend the days chronicling all the ways you let them down.

These aren't conversations, you see, *that* would just be crazy. Crazy . . . Just . . . I replay memories of conversations from when she was little, or a teenager. Those safe memories still hurt, but while I'm in them, I can see her smiling, see her eyes shining. The ephemeral recordings of my mind. If I don't repeat them, they'll fade. Eventually they'll go away.

I said, *Do you miss me?* And that was a new question, so there was no answer.

Do you remember that time you begged me to make you pancakes covered in Halloween candy one year and you got so sick? Why did I ever agree to . . . I wiped your face down with that little pumpkin hand towel, the one with the single-tooth grin. They always draw cartoon characters with friendly smiles and slightly worried eyebrows. Like they want to be your friend and they're afraid you'll mock them. You asked me while I was cooking the pancakes, "What's she worried about?" and I said she was a happy pumpkin, maybe she was just on the verge of tears, she was so happy. And you said, "People cry when they're happy? Do you cry?" I do. Lord, I do. And you told me whenever I had to cry, to just "remember the bottom of my face with a smile so maybe the top part forgets to be sad."

I hadn't thought of that in years. I wonder if I still have that towel . . .

Are you scared now, wherever you are? I hope not. I hope you remember that I love you.

The old conversations weren't coming. This was just me talking to her. My eyes were heavy and . . . you ever get so tired you can just feel your skin begging to let you sleep? I was there.

As my eyes closed, someone whispered, *"Yes."*

My hands instinctively reached to my ears to pull out headphones that weren't there, that's how close it sounded.

Then my cellphone beeped. One new voicemail. But the phone hadn't rang. Anonymous number.

I bolted out of bed. All I could think of was horror movies. Is this the part where I was supposed to run out of the house or stay inside? Don't play the voicemail, I knew that much. I ran outside, and jammed the phone into my mailbox. I left it locked up there, convinced the next day's sunlight would make it safe to listen to the message, or maybe the voicemail would vanish as mysteriously as it came. I went back inside, closing and locking every door as I got to the bedroom, keeping whatever was in the other rooms out of my room. It was too dark to watch the sheets now, too dark to watch the air. So I watched the clock projecting on the ceiling.

A whisper poured through the gap under the door,

from around the corner, down the hallway. "Start again." Then closer, "Start again." A command, an offer. "Start again. Start again. Start again." Many voices, or one voice doubled and trebled.

I couldn't move my legs. Even when the whispers got louder, even when the footsteps started, like a thousand, thousand ants dancing across sandpaper rushing at me under the doorframe. The noise built into a hiss of insect wings, into the rush of air, into the noise of TV static like a long breath being drawn in, whispering, *I can't see*, over and over, panicked and desperate, and somehow familiar. *I can't see I want to start again.* Could you recognize a loved one by the sound of their whisper?

I called out Dee's name. I don't know why. I felt so alone here, and she was dead and gone, but also trapped in a recording of some long-ago night in the desert. Years ago, but here again, somewhere. I said her name, gently, the way I would call her when I wanted to surprise her with ice cream.

The whispering stopped. Everything stopped. No footsteps, all of it hovered in the background, interrupted. I felt a presence, like a pale creature had turned its attention to me. An eyeless woman with frizzy hair and a mud-stained tank top, pale legs veined purple and blue— why did that come into my head?—waiting for me to continue. I called out Dee's name again. Shadows rippled across the light in the crack under the door. Did I remember to lock it? Liquid black fingers probed underneath, clutching through the doorjamb, a shadow trying to pull itself into the room.

Something paced in front of the door. Another probing shape like a long, slippered foot. The doorknob rattled, the lock turned.

And *then* my eyes closed.

I hadn't fallen asleep. I saw the shadow. Then I was in blackness. Then my eyes opened. One long blink, click-click.

Sharp knives of sunlight stabbed through the blinds, cutting through the dust. My house was my house, but now it *wasn't* my house, because she'd come home. I didn't see her, couldn't hear her, not at that point, but I knew she was there. I didn't want to call her name. I'd spent last night praying for daylight. I couldn't invoke her now. Walking around, I'd get the sense she left the room just before I came in, that she was around the corner of the doorway, just out of sight. Listening to me. Waiting for me. For something.

The bedside drawer was open and empty. The kit was on the floor, still neatly tied up in its little leather roll. I have photos of her lining the hallway. Some of them were on the floor, face down. I might have done that in my stumbling urgency to lock down last night. I broke and called her name, convinced she would answer, certain if I didn't call it out, this invisible tether, however I'd pulled her from her Point A to my Point B, would snap and she'd disappear. I was terrified of finding her in the house, terrified of losing her all over again.

I made breakfast and left a plate out for her, a big pile of toast like I used to make when she was little. Four slices arranged in a diamond on a paper towel. I swear she survived from her fifth birthday to her tenth on buttered toast alone. I didn't want to leave and I couldn't stay.

Daylight meant it was safe to get my phone from the mailbox. I checked myself in the mirror by the front door, tidied up just enough to downgrade from horrifying recluse to mama-didn't-get-enough-sleep. I pulled the phone out and turned it on. One message, caller ID said Anonymous. I spun around, looked back at my house, watched the way the light and air played at the curtains. Was something in there? Had anything changed?

I thought somehow playing the message via speakerphone would help prevent demonic trickery, even though nobody else was around to hear. There was a long pause. Rattling noises. A key sliding into a slot. And another pause.

"Ash, Ms. Esperanza, sorry I was trying to navigate putting down coffee and breakfast and drive, you know how it goes. Hey, it's Campbell Parker, hey, I just wanted to touch base with you because of how we left things yesterday. I didn't mean to uhh . . . I mean, you were upset when you left, and it just made me wonder if it was anything we said or did, or . . . can I get you coffee? Can we meet? I just want to talk a few things over with you to finalize your bit on *The Memory Show*, and then maybe . . . I don't know. If you want to talk, you know? I'm . . . well, anyway, call me back . . . " And then her number, which I won't give you, because god knows she doesn't need it anymore. Don't need anyone leaving her messages.

We set a coffee date for . . . it was the start of today, actually. Is it still today? It was, it was today at the start of today, but at some point it became three days later, which was the next time I'd see Campbell, but I think . . . I think *today* is still today. Somehow. Sorry. Let me explain.

We met at my local coffee shop. It's out of the way enough that the only people who might recognize me are locals, and they mostly don't care who I am. I love this space, an old arched roof warehouse converted into a café. The place was covered in art. They had one of my pieces mixed in there. The photographer called it *The Raging Bull*. I'm in a Greek Dress in Central Park performing *Call to Action*, one breast exposed, my arm flexed, fist clenched, as I'm shouting at this policeman who's coming at me with a coat to cover me up. But uhhh . . . where am . . . was I? The walls in the coffee shop are seafoam green, painted with murals of large fish and squids and stuff that reached up onto the arch of the exposed wood ceiling. It normally brought an odd sense of calm, somewhere deep and dark and quiet, and most of all, safe. Today it set me at unease, like I was being forced to sit in the bottom of a swimming pool. I nodded to the barista and they started working on my regular.

Campbell was there when I arrived, sitting on one of the old, battered couches with a small box at her feet. She had a small black bag, zippered up and covered in tiny pockets. I guessed correctly that it was a recorder, but we'll get to that.

She chose to start with honesty, which wasn't at all what I was expecting. "I know who you are."

You can imagine, any conversation that starts this way would put you on guard, right? I don't want to . . . God it feels so egotistical to talk about being famous, but doing what I've done, I'm used to hearing people say they know me. I've heard it too many times to count, and enough to know that her tone was different. I saw her face twist up a little. A question back there, something she'd been rehearsing for a day, something that wasn't going as smoothly as she'd hoped. I tried to cut her off at the pass, make this easy. "You're going to ask to interview me, aren't you?"

"I know you're Dee Bolan's mother. Please hear me out for a minute."

"Are you recording this?"

"I want to. Obviously, not trying to hide it. But I'm not . . . it's not *for* anything. Not yet."

"So either way, you get an interview or you get audio of me freaking out and yelling at you before I storm out of here, right? Win-win?"

"None of this . . . god, I have a show, I do a podcast called *Salton Signal*. Full disclosure."

"Full disclosure usually comes before the invite for coffee."

"I'm not. I promise. Just give me two minutes. I've been exploring that area for over a year now. Well, not like . . . crawling around out there, but I've been studying it. Everything that's happened. Dee, Sharon, they aren't the only ones to disappear. And *you* know what I mean, right? Disappear? Like, Dee came back from the sea the first time, but she wasn't there, right? Not entirely?"

I leaned forward on the sofa a little. "I always used to tell Dee that . . . I guess that's true of anywhere you go. Whether something good or bad happens, the *you* that comes back shouldn't be the same *you* that left. Otherwise what's the point of the trip? Every decision changes us, even the choices we don't make. Most of the time we don't notice it, but the people around us do. You don't think that echoed around my brain every day I woke up after she came back the first time?"

"It's a profound way to look at it."

"Stop."

"I'm sorry?"

"Whatever this . . . " I waved my hands all around. "Whatever this is, what you're trying to do. Stop. You have something you want to ask, ask it."

"Look, a lot of other shows that have covered the . . . What am I saying, I know you probably know all of the . . . uh . . . sorry. I'm trying to cover everything that's happened in the area, the testing at Slab City, the military experiments, the abandonment, land rights, water acts, the creation of the Salton Sea, the collapse, the Anza Borrego lights, and yeah, the crack in the sky, all of it is meshed together. There is something bigger happening in the desert. One thing is tied to the next. Two weeks ago I went out there to explore for our latest episode. There's this huge art installation by the shoreline, a weathervane covered in stained glass. Anonymous artist just built the whole thing overnight. Nobody knows where it came from. I mean . . . it's not a mystery, it's art, but it's one of those . . . never mind. This thing though, it pointed back at a house in Bombay Beach. But not in a way . . . God this will sound crackpot, but . . . the wind wasn't blowing the right way for this to happen."

"You don't think it was fixed in place?"

"No. It moves. Moved. It just stopped when I touched it."

"Then it wasn't windy enough that day or something."

"You don't have to believe me. But it pointed straight over the floodwall at this shiny airstream trailer parked next to an abandoned house. Like *the* house. The one Dee mentioned in her journals. The trailer was open, so I peeked inside. Found those dictabelts. Suddenly, as part of my regular day job stuff helping Kfira, you cross into my life. And something on those recordings affected you."

"The whirlpool."

"What's that?"

I shrugged and motioned for her to continue.

"I don't know if you've ever been to the Salton Sea—"

"Fuck no."

"Okay, ha, yeah. But the box those Dictabelts came in was just . . . neat, and crisp and didn't quite belong there. Across the top it had the name Raymond Wood stenciled in blue. Backwards, you know. Wood, Raymond. Military style. I didn't even notice the name on the box until after you'd left. We've been listening to them on repeat since you left the studio. I heard birds, and you didn't. Nobody else did. And then you come along, and you hear the name Raymond Wood, which none of *us* have heard . . . you didn't see the box when you came in, right? Maybe you read the name and forgot?"

I shook my head, staring out the window. I know I'd seen it before, but not there. I couldn't remember.

"You know I haven't done a real interview since . . . I don't know. Hearing you say that earlier—*Dee Bolan's mother*." I shook my head. I was like a coiled spring, ready to fly off the couch, out the door and into traffic. "Until she went to the Salton Sea, I was Ash Esperanza, artist. Then everything happened and I was Aisling Bolan, if I was lucky. And I was . . . lucky, I guess, that Dee survived her first trip out there. Because then I was Ash Esperanza, mother of Dee Bolan, crazy desert lesbian. But Dee was still alive. When she left us, people had mostly forgotten her story. Her death was a footnote on the news. And I couldn't talk about it to anyone without tearing my guts out for the world to watch. People always debate separating the art from the artist, but nobody would separate Dee's tragedy from my life. It was . . . when I was using . . . when I had my troubles, that was months of people just reminding me that I was a junkie, or worried I was going to relapse, and I got that under control, right? All I wanted was to break free and get back to making things, but people kept pushing my face down into it. I couldn't make art anymore."

Did I remember to breathe? Was I still breathing?

"And this time, losing her, anything that came out was her, an attempt to reach her, or apologize to her, or be angry with her. Nobody else needed to hear it or see it. Nobody else deserved to. I didn't need them pushing her in my face to remind me. Ash Esperanza had to go away because keeping her alive was keeping Dee's death alive. And . . . I guess what I'm trying to say is I have little interest in unburying any of it. I wanted to elevate her. I wanted to disappear and lift her up. That's why I made my last project. My *last* project, you understand? Whatever it is you're trying to do, I won't be part of it. Thanks for the coffee, hope you got what you came for, and you can turn that thing off."

She actually did. I doubted it was the only recorder she had running, but at least she was making a show of respecting my wishes. "It's been . . . a few years since Dee passed? Since Susan found them out there?"

"Six. Almost."

She folded her arms across her stomach. "Susan stopped talking to me. I guess . . . I said full disclosure, right? The whole reason I started this podcast, looking into everything that happened out there is because . . . like you said, the Susan that left wasn't the Susan that came back. She was this tough little ray of sunshine, this pure, happy soul. She found them out there—"

"She didn't find *them*."

"Yes. Dee's body. When she came back . . . it was like someone took a lightbulb and coated the inside with coal dust. Like . . . you think you know someone and . . . we were friends. We were really good friends. Last text of the night friends, and this is the weird part, she never talked about . . . I didn't know she had a sister. We talked all the time and she never mentioned Sharon."

I didn't know what to say, but I knew enough to not say anything. Either we were both drowning in the same pool and this is how we breathed, or she was lying, trying to wring something out of me.

"Did you ever talk to Susan?"

I shook my head.

"I want to know what happened to my friend."

"Did you ever consider it's not your place to find out? That you could just offer quiet support and let her find her own way through?"

"Has quiet support from friends worked for you?"

"It's different."

I saw her eyes dance down to my left arm. I followed them, noticed a tiny bruise near another tiny bruise. Tried to be nonchalant as I rested my hand there to hide them.

If she noticed, she didn't show it. "I definitely wasn't implying that you were . . . I don't want this to happen to anyone else. I want people to know what happened. When she first got back from the desert, Susan was . . . I don't know, cordial? Asked for time to herself, and we definitely gave it to her, all of her friends. But then she just kept on drifting. Farther and farther out, and no matter what I tried, she wouldn't talk to me. Not a word."

"That's her right."

"I know. But . . . just a *hello*. Just a word so I know she's okay? Who knows the rules to these things? You see people pulling away, what's the right thing to do? Keep supporting them, but don't try to force them to talk, and what am I supposed to do? I want to figure out what happened. What *is* happening. For me, that started with Susan. That led me to your daughter and Sharon. Then I started discovering other things. They're not the only people that have been affected. Just the highest profile, I guess. I don't want anyone else to . . . you've never thought about going out there?" She swallowed the question, bit down on its tail as it escaped her mouth, but now it was out in the wild.

"I never had a reason. The first time, they brought Dee to a hospital. I rushed to her side and stayed with her. Why would I need more than that? The second time, she was at the coroner's office. Why would I need to see more than that? She's gone. But she's not, is she? Can't you leave me alone to figure that out?"

"Of course." She stood up and gathered her bags. "I'm really sorry to have . . . if I bothered you."

"You did. But if you're telling the truth about knowing Susan, I understand why you did."

"You think I'm—no. You say Dee is haunting you? I believe *you*. Has anyone said that to you since any of this happened? Has anyone asked you how you were feeling? I just wanted to know. I wanted you to have a chance to tell the world. That it's not suicide if . . . Jesus, I'm sorry I don't mean to take it there, but *none* of this is her fault or your fault or . . . I understand if you don't . . . you know, I never should have asked, that was selfish. I'm sorry. I really am."

Her hand danced forward, then back, looking for a handshake, adjusting her bag strap. I didn't move. I let her flounder, then looked down at my coffee. She got the idea and left.

"Everything okay?" The barista came by with a refill and a muffin. She knew my routine. I nodded and she smiled at me as she left. My phone pinged a minute later. Another voicemail. Another anonymous number. Campbell must have felt pretty bad for herself. Good. I placed the phone face down. It buzzed again as I went to take a bite of my muffin. Then four more times. Four new messages. All anonymous. Campbell was in tatters. Well deserved.

I shook my head and plugged in my earbuds. I didn't need anyone else here listening to this. I hit play on the first voicemail. It sounded like a big room, if there's . . . can you tell that from audio? It sounded big. And then, yeah, people walking. Campbell must have butt-dialed me walking away from the shop, but this didn't sound like LA sidewalks. More like someone standing in loose dirt and spinning around on their heel really slowly. Then I heard another noise, like clapping, and then the message cut off.

I hit play on the second message, and it was an intense droning, like . . . an old electric guitar, if you grab the metal thing on the cord from the amplifier? The plug? And it just kind of *HHMMMMMMM* hums like that?

Message three. Wind blowing. Another butt-dial. Over a minute long, according to the screen. I listened. Don't you always listen to butt-dial messages? Hoping you'll hear some secret part of life sneak out, a private side someone doesn't want you to know about? I smiled. There was a quiet *tick*, like someone had dropped a stone far back in a marble hallway, too clean to make sense. Like, you'd need a recording of a stone in a hallway playing over the wind . . . you get it. Then came two *ticks*.

I must have looked like a confused puppydog, head tilted, lips parted, leaning in closer to the phone as if it would somehow help me hear better. My face was warped and reflected in the screen. The table smelled like dust and coffee and old paper. The noise repeated. *Tick-tick*. It kept going, getting further away, way down a dank hallway, around a corner in a room with shattered walls and peeling paint, stinking of decay and stagnant salt water. I saw it in my mind, and I heard her clear as a bell.

I do. I miss you. Oh, that silly pumpkin. I haven't thought of it . . . I don't remember the . . . I remember feeling sick when I saw it because of eating all that candy . . . Why would you even agree to make that? Were you trying to teach me a lesson?

She laughed her beautiful rolling laugh, and the coffee shop filled with icy water. I was cold to the bone, couldn't breathe. People were ordering coffee and drinking and talking while I drowned in front of them. Empty static scratched my ears. Dee was waiting for something. Was I supposed to speak? Had I already? The pause felt like hours, but it was the exact time it took me to talk about that stupid towel last night.

Why would you . . . why would I be scared?

"You're hearing this, right?" I said to nobody. In the screen, my reflection was aghast, eyes watery, jaw open.

Where am I now? Where am I now? Why would I be scared . . . Why would I be scared? Are you sleeping? Don't sleep! Should I be scared? Should I? WHY WOULD I BE SCARED? WHY?!

My lungs felt empty. Worse than empty. Dry-heaving, bucking, fluttering useless plastic bags. The room snapped blackout/lights up and I bolted straight up, hands scrabbling, chest heaving. I was drowning. Suffocating. My hair waved in front of my eyes like seaweed, clinging to eyelashes and invading my nostrils. Something pinned me down. Why was I the only one who knew the room had filled with water? Why wasn't anyone else . . . where was everyone else? A hand reached through the murk and seized my face, turning me, clamping my nose shut.

The barista, pinching my nose. My lungs kicked once, twice. I felt like I was going to vomit, then everything kind of tumbled back into place. My mouth dropped open and I drew in a long breath. I locked eyes with her and she eased up, holding my wet cheeks in her palms.

"I pinched someone's nose shut once to snap them out of a bad trip. Sorry, I didn't know what else to do. Are you okay? Are you prone to seizures?"

I was on the floor. The iron grip on my arms relaxed as I looked around. Everyone in the coffee shop had rushed over, surrounding me, protecting me from myself. And I felt . . . embarrassed . . . or loved? So many bodies around me, all reaching to me, all so concerned. Nobody had touched me like this since Dee passed, since the last hug at her funeral. That might have been my last human contact. Mostly by my choosing. We sat in silence like a Renaissance painting, huddled on the floor in a loose circle, everyone's hand on someone else's shoulder or arm or leg. I swiped tears from my cheeks.

They all insisted on helping me to my chair. The barista wrapped an arm around me and yeah, maybe I leaned into her more than what would be normal. Is there normal in a situation like this? It was human contact and I needed it. I hadn't been touched in years, I think. I guess it could sound creepy, but I just . . . hadn't allowed myself to reach out. Someone reached out to me.

"Have you had episodes before?" Her hair smelled like fruit shampoo.

I'm sorry were the only words I could make, so I held to them, over and over, pushing my raft closer to shore. Someone in the coffee shop was using words like *stroke* and *heart attack* and *seizure*. That was enough to snap me back to reality. I told him . . . *told* is probably understating it . . . told him I wasn't that old. I was fine. But I couldn't tell anyone why I was crying.

"I just need a minute. I think I spilled my coffee . . . " I laughed at the barista, squeezed her hands tightly. There was something on her face. Empathy, maybe. Or embarrassment at the way everyone in the coffee shop stared. We were so close her eyes were doing that thing where they locked onto my eyes individually, left-right-left-right, the kind of thing you usually only see at the end of first dates or when someone is trying to find a way to give you bad news. She touched my shoulder and I kissed her on the cheek. I wanted more. I don't know why, that would have been weird. On so many levels. It would have . . . ugh.

"Okay. Let's just . . . get you comfortable. I'm sorry. I'll get you another. You sit." She guided me down on the sofa and swiped the table a couple times, then hustled away. I folded into myself, keeping my eyes down. My phone was face-up on the table, still playing, the progress bar onscreen crawling forward like an inscrutable divine instrument. My earbuds dangled over the edge of the table, a suicide victim swinging back and forth as ghostly voices and sounds poured out. I heard a girl's voice singing, *she is my stars and moon . . .*

I clicked the phone into sleep mode. The barista came back with a new coffee in a to-go cup, muffin in a bag. Message received.

"I should go. But would you mind . . . could you listen to this for me?" I held the earphones out to her. "My . . . someone left me a message, and I can't quite make out the number. Do you mind? I don't want to play it on speaker. Privacy, you know."

The barista nodded and pressed the earbud against her ear. She smiled at me, her eyes darting to her coworker behind the counter. *Be ready to move, we have a live one . . .*

I hit play again, watched the slider tick off the seconds. She cocked her head a little, then looked at me and shook her head. "Is this the right message? I can't hear anything." She held the earbud out to me, and I could hear Dee's voice asking, *Where did you go? Where are you?*

Cognitive dissonance is a hell of a thing. Two of us experienced two different *whens* at the same time. I mean, I guess that's life, but this was . . . if we both sat down to watch a dog walk across the street, we'd experience it differently, but we'd objectively agree there was a street and a dog.

"I need to go home. They'll call back if it's important, I guess." I looked at her, lower lip trembling. "But I don't want to go home." I took her hand. "She's *there*, do you understand?" My chin shook so hard I had to pretend to scratch it. "You didn't lose her, I did. My daughter is . . . Dee was so . . . it became so *public*. I had to lose her again and again. When the police came. When insurance called. When the press poked around. Years later when it became some kind of fun home game for the internet crowd. Then it was months, and then years where nobody asked about her, and that burned too. All I wanted was someone to talk to. And the Sea swallowed her. The greedy . . . *thing* out there is holding everything close to its chest. But she keeps . . . There's two ways your children come back, and they both hurt. You get memories of happy times, and those twist your stomach. Or, you replay everything you did wrong in your mind. That's my day-to-day, regrets, things I could have done better. When she was still around, and I'd worry to her that I could have done more for her, she used to tell me she turned out okay, *I turned out all right ma*, I heard that a lot. But I didn't believe her. Because I *could* have done better. If I had, she would have come to me before she went back out there. I just needed to take the edge off. Just needed some . . . I don't mean to bother you. Oh, God please tell me this doesn't mean I need to find a new coffee spot, I'm just having a really, really bad—"

"Do you need me to call you an uber? On the house? You can sit for a few minutes if you need to. I'm not trying to chase you out, really. You're one of our best regs. I thought you'd want to . . . you know, you'd want privacy?"

My hand floundered against my side, bouncing, squeezing my leg, my purse, making fists. "No, I can walk it. I'll walk it." I grabbed the coffee and muffin. "I lost my daughter."

"I'm so sorry." The barista touched her heart.

"It's been years. But it never is, you know? Have you ever—no. You know, I'm sorry. I'm . . . this is a bad day. I'll be back. I'm allowed to come back?"

"Of course!" She smiled and helped me up.

I left the coffee shop, eyes on the ground. I made it a few blocks and had to catch my breath. Everything was spinning. My arms tingled. I needed to stabilize. Get home and stabilize. Responsibly. I started to toss the coffee and muffin, then decided to leave them on the ground next to the trash can in case a homeless person came by. Then *that* felt insulting and stupid so I put them on top of the can instead. I apologized to the trash can and kept walking. My phone vibrated in my pocket. I refused to look at it.

The windows in my house were dark. Too dark, like the inside of the house was swallowing light. I went to my car and sat inside, placing the phone on the car charger. Seventeen new messages. I wasn't going to check. It was only nine-thirty in the morning. I brought up a map, plugged in a destination.

I yanked the phone from its holster and texted Campbell: *I'm going now. Right now, because if I don't I never will. If you can be at the North Shore Yacht Club by four-thirty, I'll talk to you there.*

I didn't wait for a response. I started driving, afraid to turn on the radio, afraid to have the audio on the GPS for directions. I was afraid to check mirrors, afraid to see anything reflected in glass, afraid to do anything but drive. The L.A.-grey skies faded and shifted to a sun-faded robin's egg as I got away from the city and deeper into the desert. I kept my eyes on the horizon, searching for a crack, a flash at the corner of my eye. In the city, the endless whooshing and rumble of other traffic was a handy distraction. Now in the desert, the car filled with uncomfortable silence.

My phone beeped. Another new message. About every ten miles, it would add another, then another. All anonymous. I left the 10 Freeway and passed through the town of Mecca. Had this become some kind of pilgrimage? A sign from heaven? Then I passed by the International Banana Museum. Signs everywhere.

"Who thought any of this was a good idea?" I muttered, looking out the window. "The . . . living out here, I mean. Who am I talking to?"

The exit signs and landmarks taunted me. There was a sign for the North Shore Museum, a giant building that had been born a Yacht Club, and rotted into a dilapidated building that became Dee's breaking place. Now it was a bright shiny museum, twice ephemeral. A wave of cold shot through the car. I shuddered, thinking I had just run over the spot in the road where they were found the first time. Dee and Sharon, half-naked and freezing while I was at home.

I had a few more miles to go for Bombay Beach, the place where Dee's misadventure started and where her life ended years later. I'd read online that it was growing into an artist's commune, flowers and trees growing over an ancient battlefield. The sea lurked on my right like a silent, empty mouth, wet and open.

The A/C was off, but the glass against the back of my hand was freezing. I checked the dashboard. Eighty-two degrees. I rolled down my window and stuck my hand outside. The car filled with the low Doppler-*whop* of wind. My hand sliced through the air, but it felt more like cutting through the surface of a very still, very cold lake. I rolled the window back up. Bombay Beach was the next exit.

The phone rang. Anonymous. I let it go to voicemail. Or I tried. The ringtone paused every twenty seconds, then started again. I was close enough that I didn't need the map, so I took the phone off the charging cradle and threw it into the glovebox. I slowed down and signaled, turning off of the highway down Avenue A and heading toward the sea. I couldn't see the water from the street. I remembered that they had to build a wall at the edge of the little town after a disastrous flood took out a bunch of beachfront property. I rolled down a long stretch of nothing just off the highway, then a few trailers began to pop up, then this—bar? Hotel? I don't know—called the Ski Inn, some faded remnant of the glorious past that looked like it was still functioning as . . . something.

I suppose a semi-abandoned town is another type of recording. It's hard to describe without making it sound like I'm passing judgment on the people who live here. All of the ramshackle houses, the trailers that look like they'd turn to rusty powder if you sneezed at them, the little tetanus temples and junkie joints. There was life and glory here once. Hope. Ambition. Most long-time residents would tell you hubris killed the sea. This town lived another life that nobody would believe if it hadn't been recorded.

I'm basically paraphrasing a pamphlet at this point. I've learned most of the history as I lay here bleeding in the museum. It wasn't a museum when I came in. Has someone found me yet? I mean, not now, obviously, I'm still here watching everything fall apart, but you. You. Listening, or reading the transcript, are you there? Did any of this happen if you're not there? Anyway. We're almost to *here* now. Here, where I am.

Where was I, though? Driving into Bombay Beach, right? I tried to lock the doors as subtly as possible, convinced from the outside it sounded like a gunshot, huge neon letters above my car saying I DON'T TRUST YOU. I was driving along the big dirt wall at the end of the road. The sea was just beyond, but I felt like it was behind me. Around me. Over my shoulder.

I turned left at the end, because that's all you could do. There were muddy ruts and standing water, but nothing too difficult for my SUV to handle. I saw little signs here and there among the graffiti and destruction, artists reclaiming spots, free to explore their large-scale weirdness in the desert, away from the prying eyes and high rents of Los Angeles. Creation in constant battle with decay.

I parked on an empty patch of dirt and stared out of the window. Behind me, the sea. To the right a dilapidated house, to the left, a collapsing two-story house, and in front of me, an old airstream trailer, just like Campbell had said, parts of it still shining silver. One of these kids was not like the other. The houses appeared to have been overrun by alternating waves of meth heads and street artists. Garbage littered the property. Broken . . . *everything*. Furniture. TVs. Computer screens. Appliances, kitchen sinks, sofas, tires, clothes, shopping carts, you name it; thrown in, piled around, and somehow, among all of that, art. Beautiful murals on the wall, paper paste-ups and just . . . it was amazing.

There was a strange kaleidoscope effect, utter disaster from the street, and closer up, the art, and in between, all of these jagged, graffiti scribbles, little remembrances, cries for help, signatures bragging of who got there first covered by signatures of others who felt more deserving. Life over life over life, all existing simultaneously and separately.

I wanted to find the orange marker, the bright orange that Sharon and Dee saw. *You will hear their voices when you try to sleep.* This had to be the house. One of them, anyway. But that trailer . . .

I opened the door and warm air poured in. The temperature seemed to be back in agreement with the thermometer. I held my breath and turned on the radio, scanning through the channels, end to end, pausing on any weird static noises, switching bands to AM, back to FM, hoping for a sign or a warning. Nothing.

Three drops of water smacked the windshield. The sky was clear. Two more drops. Then another, inside the window, trickling down the rearview mirror, rolling around its edge, cutting loose and smacking the dashboard above the glovebox, running down to the gap and then inside. And then another, and another. Two more hit my arm, ice cold like needles, so cold I could feel them coming out the other side. More drips from above, all flowing into the glovebox. I climbed out of the SUV and walked to the edge of the property. My keys jangled heavily to alert sleeping meth heads, clipped to my belt loop with a canister of pepper spray. As I got closer I couldn't decide if the safest thing was to make more noise or to stay quiet.

I found myself drifting toward the airstream. I walked a wide circle around it. It looked like it had dragged itself from the bottom of the Salton Sea, an aquatic beast come to shore laden with the eggs of lost memories and things forgotten, crawling all this way to lay them far from water, safe from predators. And it had failed.

I'm sure that sounds dramatic, but if anything I'm understating things. The windows on the side of the trailer were caked in white, salty grime. A few boxes pressed up against the glass, pushing yellowed, sun-faded curtains into strange shapes. Things moved against the glass, bugs maybe? Or fish, swimming in shallow tide pools?

The airstream was torn open like a monster had pushed its way through a primordial metallic sac to crawl screaming into the world. Its innards spread across the surrounding scrubby dirt patch, the human hyenas and carrion birds of the desert having picked it clean. Stained yellow foam insulation spilled onto the ground, mixing in the dirt and clinging to the plants nearby. Broken shards of glass and plastic, shreds of linoleum in avocado green and puke yellow like shattered bones drifted in the desert scrub. There was a rusty chair, and someone had not-so-helpfully propped up a filthy, broken doll in the seat, one eye glued shut with mud, the other staring blankly into the distance. It had one chubby hand raised in greeting. Someone had written SHE'S NOT HERE across her forehead in red sharpie.

Something inside caught my eye, just under her chair. It was a brand-new-from-decades-ago mp3 player in one of those blister packs that slices your hands to shreds when you try to open it. A big sticker emblazoned across the front, slightly faded, proclaimed the device as *Y2K READY*!

I took it. Why would you take something that doesn't belong to you from a place you don't belong? It felt like the right thing to do. Like it was . . . well, now I know why. At the time, though, no clue. Have you read Dee's journals? If you're hearing this? It was her favorite thing, I think. This wasn't the same brand as her mp3 player. This *was* hers. Had been, or would be, I don't know the right verb for it. This was getting part of my daughter back.

That doll kept staring at me with one good eye, the letters on her head burning like neon fire: SHE'S NOT HERE.

So she could be here, in my hand. I wanted to open the mp3 player. *Want* is a light word. I had a burning urge, an understanding that I would start to hear properly if I could just get into that package. I yanked at the packaging. Got my little knife out and hacked away until the plastic gave, and of course I put a nice cut across the top of my hand and the inside of my wrist. Across the street instead of down the road. Maybe you see where this is going. I pulled out the player and earphones along with some AA batteries in shrinkwrap. Nice of them to include, but I was sure they'd be long dead.

I peeled the protective cover off the screen, popped in the batteries, and flipped the power switch. The little black and white screen came on, listing ten tracks:

- GIVE YOUR AYES
- SEARCH THE SKY 33.34577522389917-115.72927096877436
- FRAGILE
- SHE WILL BRAKE YOU

BENEATH THE SALTON SEA

- WILLCOME
- LET THEM
- MAJESTY/MAJSTY/E CHO
- G396+RX MECCA CA AREA .NULL
- SPINDRIFT E/CHO FADE
- THE ETERNITY OF ETERNITIE

Some of these things used to come preloaded with demo tracks. Some of the tracks read like a set list from a typical indie band you'd find at the end of the millennium. But the typos and weird spacing, like someone didn't quite know how to save things to the device. I plugged in the earbuds and pushed them into my ears. The monochrome screen was impossible to see in the sunlight. I shaded it, seeing the faint outline of a giant battery icon with an exclamation point blinking.

Then I noticed my wrist. My hand, shiny and red. I had nothing to fix this. I started walking back to the SUV. My heart pounded in my ears, the thunder and gravel-crunch of every footstep amplified by having my ears plugged. A hiss rose under everything. It wasn't static. It was gentle, pulsing, cooing. *Shh, shh, shh. Everything's going to be okay.*

The screen displayed an inverted triangle with a circle inside. The circle was half black and half red, this on a screen not capable of displaying color. Below the triangle, thick block letters read TAC 52. I took the earphones out and jammed the player back in my pocket. They continued to hiss, a tiny snake warning me, or luring me. I walked toward the house on the left. I looked at my wrist. Grey and white and black TV fuzz flowed down my palm and fingers. Everything was fine.

I stopped and sat in the dirt, pulling off my shoe. I took my sock off and tied it around my wrist until I felt my heartbeat there. I was sure that fixed it.

I looked up at the house. There was a shadow on the

second floor. I should explain that it probably used to be a two-story thing, but time or vandals or something had knocked all but two of the walls down upstairs. The shadow waved at me. It was a woman. She was skinny and small, wearing shorts and cowboy boots, her hair pulled into some odd configuration that shone white as the sun passed through her.

Her voice echoed in a way that didn't make sense. Like she was shouting into a tin bucket. "We need to talk. If you feel like crying, these aren't the kind of places you should be taking deep breaths in, if you get me. So come on up top where there's air soon as you're ready."

The front door was folded over on itself, a large chunk of ceiling pinning it in place and blocking access. The garage door was still hanging in there, every panel punched out so it looked like an empty spreadsheet. It was propped open by the remains of a sofa. I crouched low and went in. There were at least five sofas in various post-mortem stages piled near the opening. Beyond them a strange topsoil of garbage, mattresses, shattered TVs, broken plastic, porcelain, and glass on shredded carpet padding. The smell was unimaginable. Chemical, biological, painful.

I didn't know where to walk. I followed the softest path—discarded food boxes, blankets, and shredded cloth. The center of the room had been cleared, open boxes of snacks on the ground, fresh. I don't know what low point a person has hit to want to spend any of their life in a dive like this. The house, I mean, not the town. There are plenty of kind and wonderful people around the sea, real houses with yards, and people with lives, god I must sound like a snob, I'm sorry.

The walls were just . . . coated in art. It was amazing, and sad, and horrifying, and breathtakingly beautiful, all at once. There was a staircase in the back of the room, sunlight beaming down. Someone had covered the entire wall in white papier-mache, drawing an ascending design in bright orange, thousands of waves that travelled into the sunlight, each done by hand. A pile of spent orange paint markers drifted around the base of the staircase, some in plastic bags. Someone had spent an addled night or two trying to map a way out of their own head.

"It smells better up here, but not much," the woman's voice echoed down.

The stairs looked sturdy enough, so I climbed. The wood sang and screamed and popped. I emerged into a little makeshift lounge. Someone had pulled some old sofas and beach chairs up here, painted a huge circular fire pit on the floor complete with violet and teal flames. An empty frame of a big screen TV perched on the edge of the building, the screen shattered and the backing punched out so that the only channel playing was twenty-four/seven Salton Sea. Empty bottles everywhere, surgical tubing, lighters, matchbooks, spent condoms and some soldiers never called to duty. A fat porcelain ashtray sat on the ground at the edge of the fake firepit, a small pyramid of insulin needles artfully arranged within. Some of them seemed to have a little something inside. I wasn't that desperate. I don't think I was that desperate.

From here, I could see over the dirt wall that held the sea back from Bombay Beach. A few dozen yards of mud and sand over the horizon and then the sea stretched back into forever. When the wind blew the stink of the house away, it brought in the sea, stagnant and fishy. That weathervane sculpture Campbell had mentioned was there, pointing right at me. I felt a presence like eyes, dozens of people standing silently on the other side of the flood wall, heads tilted back, hands pointing out to the water. Dee is part of that sea, in the water forever.

I moved closer to the edge and whispered her name. "Dee-Bee, I'm here . . . "

It felt like . . . not the right thing to do. The only thing to do. That's how everything works out here. You think you're exploring, you think you're discovering, but you're being *led*. Something discovers you, ties an invisible filament around your neck and through your nose and you go where it wants.

"You doing okay?"

I nodded, turning slowly. I'd somehow forgotten someone called me up here.

"Anything you want to talk about?"

"Not yet."

"Come and sit." She was in a battered loveseat with her legs straight out, crossed at the ankles. Her entire body was in shadow except for bright pink cowboy boots that lay in the sunlight. Between the boots and the harsh line of darkness, her pale skin was crossed with tiny purple and blue veins. The sun pushed in just enough to catch the edges of her silver hair, the dark, wet coal pits of her eyes. Her smile. If it was a smile. "Here we are, you and I and her and them."

I glanced over my shoulder. Nobody else was here.

"We're all just different chunks of glass that fell from the same cracked sky. You're starting to see it, right?" She stood, like a corpse rising from a bog, but still submerged in the murky shadows.

"Ash, my name is—" Something clicked against the table between us, broken tree branches, skeletal fingers, it was hard to say.

A shape rose over her shoulder, another woman, hair billowing on an invisible tide. It was Dee. I don't know how I knew. I moved closer and reached a hand out, pushed into the shadow like cold water. Things swam inside that gloom, unseen, darting around and through my fingers. My shirtsleeve turned dark, wicking shadows heavy onto my sleeve. My wrist tingled. The first shadow, the smiling one, faded back while Dee came forward. Her eyes didn't seem right. Hollow and full of mud and twigs and fish bones. The Dee-shadow splashed down and ran in rivulets across the floor and over the edge of the building. The other woman walked to the edge of the shadow line.

"You can't talk to her yet. This isn't the place. My husband's name was Raymond Wood. My name is Doreen and you think I owe you an apology. You think I'm the reason you can't see your daughter no more. But you're wrong. I'm the reason you'll find her."

I followed the dark, wet trail from the shadows to the edge of the roof. There was a pond around my SUV. Water cascaded from the door seams. Things floated inside, blankets and clothes. Branches. Dead birds. Plastic tarps. Moving among it all, a flash of skin, pale blue, racing by the windshield. A hand pressed on glass and retreated into the darkness of the water. A woman. She came closer. Hair floating around her face, eyes hidden, mouth chattering open and closed like a goldfish. My knees bent of their own accord, ready to launch me down to the empty lot. I yelped, stopping myself. There was so much broken shit down there. I turned and sped down the staircase, Doreen calling out behind me.

I raced to the SUV, feet squelching in the mud surrounding the vehicle. But it wasn't wet. It just felt wet, sounded wet. I could feel my shoes sinking into the earth, but my eyes registered dry dirt. Dee floated facing away from the driver's side, one pale, bare foot pressed against the glass. Tiny fragments of fishbones and sticks poked into the arch of her foot. I tried to yank the door open, but it wouldn't move. The handle was wet with seawater. I left wet, red fingerprints down the side of the SUV.

I slapped at the window and raced around to the other side. Dee's head tilted down to look out the passenger window, lower jaw levering up and down. One eye socket was stuffed with twigs and mud. The other was hidden by her hair. I looked around to call for help, my voice strangling into hopelessness. The sky over the sea was bisected, black and starry on one side and pale purple on the other, separated by a jagged white line that spilled milky vapor into the air. Dee bumped grey-blue palms against the glass, jaw yammering. She pointed at me. At my pocket. She swam a tight circle, disappearing low, then popped up suddenly, pressing my phone against the glass, displaying the list of anonymous calls.

From my pocket, in tiny whispers, I heard her voice over the mp3 earbuds, *Hey ma. I've been trying to reach you. You're doing this all wrong. You left us and you're leaving me again.*

She dropped out of sight. The driver's side door popped open, accompanied by the sound of rushing water, dozens, hundreds of gallons pouring onto the dirt. I bent down to look under the SUV. There was no water, but the dirt had turned to mud, my nose filling with the smell of salt and dead fish and rot.

I heard a wet footstep, then another. And another. But I couldn't see her.

Slap. Slap. Squish. Coming around to my side.

On the ground in front of the SUV, bare footprints, wet, pressing down into the dirt. Turning. Walking toward the airstream, then sprinting. Something smacked against the side of the airstream like a car crash, sending it scraping back two feet, tearing a fresh scar across the ground that bled seawater. A sinkhole opened up, the trailer slowly crumpling down into the earth. An unholy scream filled the air, sending electricity down my spine, freezing me on the spot. I couldn't move, so I joined it, screaming and screaming until a bird landed on my shoulder, fluttering against my cheek, tiny claws clutching my shoulder.

I batted at it, turning my head, and there was Sharon, tongueless and bleeding, her mouth a wide O of concern, eyes purple-veined and bloodshot like a Blue Willow plate shattered on red earth. Her fingers grabbed and poked and pinched and pulled at my shoulder, hummingbird-fast. Behind her, Dee stood cold and grey and bloated, vomiting a slow trickle of water endlessly from loose blubbering lips, her hand a cold wet towel on Sharon's shoulder. I tumbled to the ground. The fluttering on my cheek continued.

It was Doreen, fanning me. I was on dry ground.

"Are you okay? Let's get you up . . . "

"What the hell is wrong with me?"

"You love her. She's gone and you want it to stop, the hurting. That's everything that's wrong and right with you. You keep searching for ways and you can't find them and it gets worse and worse and here you are. I love my Raymond. I want the same thing. I've been trying to let go for so long. And he . . . he doesn't—"

"Stop talking." Was I finishing her thought or commanding her?

"I finally heard him. I keep my radio on all the time. Thought I had accidentally found a bible show this morning, but then I recognized his voice, reading some Revelations. That's my favorite book. *And the sea gave up the dead who were in it, Death and Hades gave up the dead who were in them, and they were judged, each one of them, according to what they had done.*"

I moved back to the SUV. The driver's side door was open. Had I left it open this whole time? My cell phone sat on the seat. The glovebox was open. Everything was scattered inside. Nothing was wet. The screen showed eleven more new messages. There was a text too, from Campbell. *On my way.*

"I should go. I was supposed to meet someone. At the North Shore."

She let out a long sigh. "That's the last place I want to go. Honey, I mean *literally* the last place. There's things I need to see there, just like you. They buried it, you know. Everything that happened. Not under the ground, they just built a whole new fancy skin on top of its bones. Made it a museum, but the skeleton is still in there. The bones are the same. Everything that happened there still lives there.

It's a recording, too. They opened a door, but I don't know if it's letting things in or calling people back. I've been afraid, I guess. Like you, but now it's time."

I shrugged at her and popped open the passenger door, then walked around to the driver's side. She was already in by the time I sat down.

"You gonna close the door?"

"Can't, really. I got a thing with my arm. Just like you." She waved her hand at me.

I looked at my right wrist, the buzzing static had turned into a syrupy crust coating the sock I'd tied around it, spreading up my sleeve. I tried to make a fist. Felt like squeezing cotton. I thought about reaching across her to close the door, but I figured it would swing shut when I rolled out. I pulled out of the dirt lot and moved down the road, the dirt wall to our left filling my view. We bumped a few times and I watched the door flap around, but once I made that turn onto the road and gave it a little gas, the door swung shut. Doreen laughed at that.

I had that sensation again of people just on the other side of the wall, standing shoulder to shoulder, watching silently, turning their heads as we passed. The road felt rougher, harder to navigate. Something must have broken in the SUV. It was harder to control, harder to keep in a straight line.

"You got enough in you to make it?" Doreen smiled at me.

I made it to the highway, the sun moving lower, angling harsh silver light into my eyes. I kept my eye on the stripe on the side of the road, hoping no slow cars were ahead of me. I saw a post. Noticed I was drifting. Corrected. I jolted forward. The SUV was slowing, drifting into a turn off the road. I death-gripped the wheel and got it back under control.

"Was I sleeping?"

Doreen must not have heard me. Her head lolled with

every bump in the road. I passed a faded, dusty street sign informing me this was Marina Drive. A giant, rusting, L-shaped sign near the road advertised low prices on LOTS. I wondered if those prices had been updated in the last decade or two. A small gathering of short palm trees poked up in the desert grass surrounding a parking lot.

The sea loomed behind the building, undulating in a way that made no sense, six and eight foot swells, like someone shaking out a rug in hyper slow-motion. None of the waves hit shore. Doreen was oblivious to the tide, so I kept quiet. The road dead-ended at the Yacht Club. A car was parked in the lot, a familiar figure pacing in front of the headlights.

"Why is she here?"

"Who?"

I sped up. There was a dark black pool on the ground near the side of the road, bubbling and rising. It spit like a stuttering fire hydrant, slicking a dark black streak across the road. I was too late to adjust. We rolled across the black line and it felt like bottoming out in a deep pothole. Tooth-cracking, gut-punching. I let out a string of curse words, kept the SUV rolling, looking at the dashboard to see if any warning lights came on.

The sun was over the horizon. A wet, white line flickered in the dusky sky directly above the rotting Yacht Club. Stucco cracked, bricks crumbling, windows and doors boarded over and infested with graffiti. This isn't what's there, if that makes any sense. This was the old *when*, Dee's when. A beat-up looking sedan was parked near the door, flickering in and out of existence. Its headlights aimed at the side of the building, illuminating the word ECHO, repeating in ten-foot-tall orange paint around the building.

There was one other car in the lot, the one I spotted earlier, that was behaving like a parked car should. I opened the door and stepped out, raising a hand in greeting. I had no idea who I was saying hi to.

"What the fuck?" Campbell squeaked it out as if all the air had been sucked from her lungs. "Where were you? Where have you been?" Campbell ran up to me, almost tackling me to the ground, but stopping short and putting both hands on my shoulders to stop me. I smiled at her.

"We just . . . I wanted to see the area, Bombay Beach and everything. Before I talked to you. I thought it would help, kind of . . . I don't know, close the door? I know I'm running a little behind, but—"

"It's Friday."

I looked at her, then at the sky. She hadn't noticed Doreen. I wonder if she existed in this *when*. "You don't see that?" I pointed up at the sky.

"It's been three days since you . . . Do you need water?" Campbell started to go back to her car.

"No. Look at the sky, that's not a cloud . . . " I pointed and she grabbed my wrist.

"What happened here? Are you bleeding?"

"I'm not crazy!" My voice broke at precisely the wrong moment, like someone punched me in the chest on the last syllable and I coughed, bringing tears to my eyes. I couldn't look her in the eye. "You don't think that's strange? A little out of place?" I gestured at the building, the letters, the sky.

She held up her palms and locked eyes with me, speaking slowly. "I have spent all day handing out fliers around this area with your face because you have been texting me repeatedly asking for help. Do you remember asking me to meet you here at the museum?"

"That's not the—museum? Museum?!" I couldn't stop repeating the word as I pushed past her to the boarded-up front doors. I balled up my fist and knocked hard against the plywood. There was no noise. It felt like I'd punched a pillow made of static electricity. Campbell crouched a little like she was trying to coax a scared feral cat from under a car. Doreen had finally gotten out of the SUV, standing on the other side, looking at me from over the hood.

"Three days? Where was I? Where was I for that? You don't see this? Neither of you see this. You don't see this fucking—" I punched my hand into the static. It rippled like water, but felt like jello. I hit it again and again, watched the plywood door melt and bleed around my wrist, felt something on the other side grip me, crushing my fingers together, binding something hot around my wrist. Slowly, it pulled me closer to the building. I shrieked, trying to pull my arm back, fingers popping and grinding.

"It has me! It has me! She can't see it! You see this, right? I need your help!" I shouted at Doreen. By now, I'd sunken into the doorframe up to mid-bicep. Something inside yanked my arm and I crashed into the plywood.

"Stop!" Campbell ran to my side.

Arm-deep and my body wouldn't go through. Static sizzled hot against my skin like bacon grease. My shoulder protested, separated, and the building kept pulling. I wanted to reach a hand back to Doreen to plead for help— why wasn't she moving?—but I had to brace against the building or risk losing my arm. The thing wasn't letting up. I was going to lose it anyway. I turned and reached out.

"You're going to bleed out. Careful of the glass—" Campbell wrapped her arms around mine in a way that immobilized me. My arm was on fire, shoulder numb. My fingers felt shattered and I couldn't lift my hand. I heard a chorus of words, different voices in different places. *Dislocated. Broken. Ma? Sliced. High. My Zula. Maniac.*

I struggled to free myself. "She's still in there. It's still happening! Dee!" I wanted to push into the building again, but Campbell had me pinned. She slowly pulled me away. I lost the strength to fight her. My whole arm was coated in static electricity, glowing grey and white and black beneath my skin.

Campbell pulled her phone out, then pocketed it in frustration. "Where's your phone? Are you getting service?"

"She might have it." I gestured at Doreen by the SUV, but she was gone. "Three days? Really?"

Campbell ran to her car. "You're gonna bleed out and I have no fucking clue where the nearest hospital is. No way. Maybe there's a first aid kit inside the building."

How was she talking about me like I was the most important thing happening and also like I wasn't here at all? The plywood doors were still there, the one I punched leaking thick purple light like spilled paint. It mixed with my blood, shiny and black, painting the wood, running in streaks to a small puddle on the ground. It had teeth. It had a tongue. It had tasted me and tried to swallow me. This is what happened to Dee.

Campbell gently kicked at the edges of the plywood frame. Each time her foot made contact, there was a great cracking noise, like God turning on an amplifier for a big concert. A hum filled the air. The plywood turned into a clean, shiny glass door with a silver frame, just for an eyeblink. Most of the glass on the upper part of the frame was shattered, red streaks painting the cracks of what remained. A sheen of static cascaded down the front like a waterfall. Campbell kicked at the glass again, and then again, every bit of contact bringing that hot mic noise, feedback, static, popping, the door changing and changing and changing. She reached in carefully and felt around. Her arm disappeared into the vertical purple void.

She carefully drew her arm back and the opening rippled. She walked straight at the plywood, phasing, ragged plastic-wood-metal blockade flickering through every track of history. She pushed into it. A brief moment later, she carefully pushed the other door out. She disappeared for a moment, and then a light came on inside. The plywood doors disappeared. She was in the middle of a dilapidated hallway.

"Let's get you up. Watch the glass. Jesus, what am I supposed to tell the cops about this?"

She guided me into a chair that wasn't a chair. If I closed my eyes, I could see it for what it really was, a moldering 5-gallon bucket, full of filth. Someone had scrawled PUBLIC RESTRUM on the side in sharpie.

"I'm going to try to find a landline, call 911. Are you on something? Did you take any drugs?"

"I just miss her. I'm not crazy. You see it, right? The building? Hey, when you say three days . . . "

A noise rose from my pocket, the insect wing shuffle of repeated whispering.

Come find me. Start again. Hey ma. Hey ma. Hey ma.

Campbell couldn't hear it. This is what it wanted. This is what Dee's journals showed, her last moments with Sharon. This is what Susan, her sister, found at the sea. This is what I've been meant to do. You have to give it something. The you that goes to the sea can't be the you that comes back. Your sight to see, your ears to hear, your tongue to speak of what you saw. Sacrifice something to change your entire life. Nobody on the other side will understand and you'll never be able to explain it, but you'll be closer to complete. Satisfied to have an answer. Satisfied, not happy. Happy has nothing to do with it.

"They don't see it," I said to nobody. "Do you see it? Please tell me it's there. Tell me you see the building for what it is."

I looked down the hallway to a staircase at the end. The air filled with the rush of static. Doreen came down halfway, waved at me. Maybe it was a trick of the light, but I swear one of her eyes had gone crimson. The entire thing, white, pupils, everything, just a red, wet orb in her socket. Then, she held up a small knife.

"You dropped this. I'm just getting started. I can almost see Raymond. He kept disappearing if I closed my eyes. This way I won't even blink."

"What if this isn't real?" I asked Campbell. "Dee is gone and what if the only thing that's real right now is you and me and this building. Which one sounds crazier to you?"

"Nobody is calling you crazy. Okay? You need help. I need to find a phone . . . "

Campbell was down the hall, poking her head into doorways. Focusing on her made everything seem shiny and new. Fresh painted walls, new furniture. Purpose. Moving my focus even a fraction of an inch away snapped reality into the old Yacht Club, the before.

Cold pooled around me like water. I floated toward the staircase. Doreen ascended as I got closer. The air moved like gritty sand, scraping against me, making it hard to breathe. I climbed the stairs, into a dark hallway. Shafts of light shot down from holes in the ceiling. Neon orange lines ran along the walls, narrowing down at the end. Blue and orange light leaked out from a doorless frame. The walls were filthy, coated in dirt and black dust, but there were shapes underneath. Strange drawings and symbols.

Just like the trailer, it felt as if this entire building had been wrenched from the bottom of the sea. Something stung my foot. A splinter. I hadn't been floating. I was walking. I lost my shoe. Both shoes.

The walls in the room were coated in wires, some insulated, some with the bright copper exposed and shining in the strange orange and blue light. There was a stool in the middle of the room and a microphone in front of it. The microphone cable led to a small antique radio in the corner. Piles of plastic streamers . . . no, dictabelts . . . piled in front of it. There were windows on either side of the radio. It was like standing on the front of a ship. On my left, it was night, black as hell except for the purple ink in the sky. On my right, daylight, sepia-faded and painful. That light didn't come into the room, it was just there, like a sunny day in an aquarium.

I walked to the microphone. Adjusted it. As soon as my hand made contact with it, a long, low note played.

"Dee?"

The note droned again.

"Dee, please . . . "

Louder this time, tooth-grinding loud and low.

I waited. Then I said, "Ash Esperanza—"

Another note. The room got a little warmer. I felt a presence behind me and turned to see Doreen. Her face was a crimson mask. She had a knife loosely pinched between her thumb and forefinger.

"I can't blink anymore. I see him. Do you see him?"

Her eyelids looked like split hot dog casings, pulled into strange angles, flapping as she looked around. I understood. I held out my hand for the knife, and she gave it to me. Behind me, a man's voice.

"Aisling Bolan."

I turned, and a man was there, skinny, in a threadbare military uniform. His eyes were sunken and wild, and his mouth looked punched-in like a rotten apple doll. All of his teeth were gone, but not pulled. Like he'd hammered them out himself. He stood a little straighter and leaned toward the microphone. Waiting for me.

I stepped up and looked at him. "Aisling Bolan." No noise. I hesitated, then said my address and phone number.

He nodded, then gestured for me to leave the room. "She's waiting for you."

An old dance tune began to play on the antique radio, and Doreen went to him, falling into his arms. "I don't know what I've done. I think we ended the world, Doreen. It's just happening so slowly. We can't stop it, and all I wanted was you, back in my arms."

They waltzed in front of the window. Or . . . some kind of old-timey dance. From my pocket, Dee's voice rose from the mp3 player.

Come to me downstairs.

I walked down the hall, foot aching from crunching on something. I traced a numb finger along the neon paint on the wall, leaving my own trail to find my way forward or back. I took the mp3 player out of my pocket and pushed the earbuds in. I heard Dee's voice, so faint I couldn't make it out. Everything was static. Everywhere was static. Maybe if I got the earbuds in deeper. I looked at the small knife in my left hand, brown and gummy with Doreen's blood.

I just needed to get the earbuds in deeper.

Hearing it all was the worst part. The hot point of that knife scraping through my ear canal until it made crackling contact with my ear drum. The final thunder as I slapped a palm against the butt of the knife to drive it home. The weird, wet squeak as I yanked it out. Was it painful? It was like nothing I'd ever felt. But had I hurt myself? I don't know.

Hey ma. I'm just down the hall.

She was so much clearer now. The floor felt like it was built on a see-saw. Each step made the building lurch, then swing the other way as I moved forward. My ears burned, my neck was hot and wet, but I heard birds singing and the static had died down to a whispering stream.

Campbell peeked out of a room. She had a phone! A real, wired . . . and she dropped it and sprinted at me. Her footsteps sounded like cotton. Like rabbits.

Hey ma? I can't stay long.

I thought I didn't have anything left inside, but Dee was out there. Campbell was the only thing in my way. She had her little black bag slung over one shoulder, so I pulled on it. I twisted her around. Grabbed her in a weird kind of hug that sent us both stumbling back into the lobby until the side of her head cracked on the sharp edge of a peeling sawhorse. When the wood made contact with her temple, when it dented her orbital bone and crushed her eye, it turned into a welcome desk, just for a second. The whole room turned into a lobby, just as long as it took me to gasp and scream. My head bounced off the floor, and it was filthy again, covered in drywall chunks and sawdust and god knows what. I got up onto wobbly legs. Campbell's legs were wobbly too, splayed on the floor at strange angles. Her eyes rolled back to whites. She kept making this sound, *unnn unnnn unnn*, like she had forgotten what she wanted to say.

Ma? You doing okay?

No, I was not.

Come outside. Come and look!

This was like when she was little. She'd find a bug in the yard, or a cloud, or just want a hug and she'd call me so urgently. There were days when that felt like work, and I always hated myself for feeling that way. I stumbled out the door. Going over that threshold felt like walking across fire. The sand by the door was blue and shining like shattered glass. Where were my shoes?

I staggered around the corner of the building and headed for the water, because I knew she'd be there. She was cross-legged in the shallows, her back to me, looking up at the sky.

"Dee? My little Dee-Bee?"

You see it—right, ma?

I nodded. I was shivering. She slapped a hand into the water by her side.

This is warmer.

I took off my clothes and slid into the water next to her, feeling sharp rocks under my feet, twigs and fishbones stabbing into my thighs. It was warmer. It felt like champagne fizz. I wanted to hug her but I was afraid to touch her.

What happened there? Your wrist?

"Nothing was making sense."

Are you using again?

I touched her shoulder.

You don't give up to escape. You give something up to get back.

"Look at me, Dee."

She turned, slopping wet hair away from her face.

Some strands still clung to her forehead, tracing wet swirls down into her empty eye sockets. She had a clump of mud at the corner of her lip. I reached up and brushed it away.

"You didn't have any right to—you could have reached out to me, to your dad, to any of us. We could have fixed this."

You could have brought Sharon back?

"You could have learned to move on! I would have helped."

I would tell you the same thing, ma. Look at us.

"Tell me what I messed up, Dee! Tell me what I did wrong!" I leaned into her, jolting at the odd feeling of her skeleton moving beneath wet skin.

Everything. You did everything wrong. You messed it all up, but you kept going. That's what you're supposed to do. Remember what you'd tell me when I was little? 'What did you ever learn from getting something right on the first try?' Is it fair, what you've done? To hold me back from where I'm going because you're more concerned with your feelings about it than where I am? That's why I asked you why I should be scared. I was worried about you. That's why I'm here now. Let me go.

"I can't. You know that. You keep coming back every day, every night. You went off to be with your wife. And I'm alone. I'm tired of it. Tired of everything. I can't make anything. If I create, and it's not about you, people call me callous. If I create and it *is* about you, they judge it, write think pieces about if I did a meaningful enough job, as if they would have any idea, or if I could have improved on anything and for fuck's sake, it's art. It's just art. It's just a stupid way for rich people to launder their money while I get to keep the lights on, right? Isn't that all it is? Isn't that all I am? What am I now that you're gone? What was I, ever?"

She flicked her chin at my wrist, tiny droplets of mud spattering across my tattoo.

Every time you wanted to try, I found a way to get to you. But you already knew, right? You already knew the right thing to do. Start Again.

I looked at the stupid tattoo, rubbing mud over it. Digging my thumb into the new set of underlines that had mysteriously appeared. I wanted them deeper, bolder. Dee wiped it clean with her cold hand. She leaned close and I took her cheeks in my hand.

"You always had nice eyes."

I still do. Just not here.

She rested her head against mine, then leaned in and kissed my cheek, which sent a shock of cold through my body. I came up gasping for air in the dark, clean lobby of the North Shore Museum. The front door was broken. Campbell was on the ground, and she wasn't moving. The phone was on the floor next to her. I have no idea if she called 911. I couldn't hear it. Her little black bag with the recorder was next to her. So I got it out and here we are.

I don't know whose batteries will last longer.

I was so sure the only way I'd be able to let go of Dee was to let go of everything. And now I don't know. If you're hearing this, or finding me, I'm sorry. I'm guessing at this point you'll find bodies, probably just me and Campbell. Doreen's gone on, Dee's gone on. I'm going to be a corpse. That's a weird thought. I mean, we all are, but I am imminently . . .

I wonder how much of this made sense. I can't hear myself. I hope this wasn't hours of me slurring and mumbling.

If I told you art was all around you, if I told you just breathing, and walking, and experiencing the world was art, would you believe it? It doesn't matter what you focus on. Growth or decay? The rust or the paint? The thing at the end or the art that creates it? It's all art, all of it. All beautiful.

I can't feel my fingers. There's enough glass left in the

door frame that I could still finish this the easy way. Dee's muddy fingerprints are on my left wrist. I found . . . can you hear that? I found a piece of paper in Campbell's bag. Clean and white, and I'm going to make something now. While I still can. If I make it out of here, maybe I'll add to this tattoo. If I don't, hey, sharpie it on me before they close the coffin lid. Start again *while you still can*. And don't stop. Make art for as long as you're alive. You already are. Witness it and be in it. What's gone isn't gone forever and what's here isn't here forever. It leaves and comes back, changed. Otherwise, what's the point of being you? Let it go and find something beautiful. Make your life a monument to a better future.

I hope you believe me that this happened. Especially if I live, Jesus . . .

Did we talk enough? Did we? Was this a mistake? All of this?

I hope she believed me that I loved her.

Love her. Desperately, and fully, and forever. All those stars in the sky. Pain to joy to pain to joy to love

to love

to love

to love

to love

We rejoined at the apex of everything in the blackness of nothing and the bright light of convergence. There were five of us there, you,

me, the mother, her daughter, her daughter-in-law. That's a sight, isn't

it? Us in the water, the three of them on shore, if you were to draw lines between us all, it would form a pentagram. That would get tongues wagging back at the Slab, I bet. The Slabbies tolerated me for

so long, and they never believed me when I told them about you and the sky. But these girls did. I didn't realize they were all getting pulled into this. We were always so

focused on the stars, and here we are forming one of our own. That was the part that fascinated me, that crossing. It wasn't death, was it? It was a stretching, a refracting, it was us seeing us seeing us, every instance of us, every possible permutation, and what a beautiful thing, what a sight! To know that we could be infinitely beautiful and horrible and abused and anointed and elevated and adored and reviled and monstrous and cruel and loving and open and alone and united and shattered and sick and healthy and all of it all at once. You always know how much I loved marine life, and I wonder if that's why you described the

one I'm thinking of, it's called the immortal jellyfish, because it doesn't really

event the way you did., like a jellyfish. I think that's the easiest way a person could approach comprehending it, but it's not close to the truth, is it? Turritopsis, that's the

the shell curve slightly different, the tentacles reaching and flowing in different directions.

die. It reaches a refraction point, returns to the birth state, grows again, everything the same, but different, compressed, then expanded,

The scariest part was preparing to see everything properly, eternally, infinitely. You can't blink. It was never a crack in the sky, it just is, it's everything, it's

everywhere, we were so limited by
our bodies, by our minds, limited by
understanding and knowing, and the
refusal to let go in wonder, in awe.
To understand now what awe is, to
understand the sheer, overwhelming
everythingness of everything. You
found me across space and time.

What was your
experience is
now mine and
mine is yours.
There was what
existed on
earth, the
separation, but
now, reunited
across the
threshold, there
isn't you, there
isn't me, there
isn't us, there
just is. Was it
me who

sacrificed my eyes,
was it you who
turned on the
machine, was it
these women who
converged at the
sea, was there a sea,
was there any of it?
Do you understand,
the you I'm speaking
to, the you who is

writing this over sixty years ago, the
you who is reading it now, do you
understand that you're already a part
of it, that you played a role in it, that
you're here in the after just as you were
there in the before? Can you release
fear, can you drop hesitation, can you
follow us here, can you lead others with
you? The sooner you understand it, the

sooner you can be free, and if you can't, can you accept our apologies while they still mean something to us? As we move further across the veil and understand more of everything, we understand less of what contained us, the need to hope, the need for

sunrise, now, now, now NOW look, look up, look through the ground and see it look now as the arc passes, this is the moment, this is the time, if not now, there will not be another when, this is what is, this is your

chance to follow, before the light closes, before the shadow fades, follow us now, look up or remain. If you're reading this, it's your last chance to find us. If you're reading this, the window has passed. If

apologies or love or decorum or manners or politics or anger or any of it. Accept us while you can. Find us while you can. The loop is closing. This is the blessing and the curse of the infinite, not all can follow, not all at once. Some must stay while others move. There are pools, there are rivers, there are deep oceans and puddles and drops and spray and this is how the universe reveals itself to us in all of its everything. Look to the sky, tonight, this afternoon, at

you're reading this,
live while you can.
We tried to help
you avoid all of
this. Everything
that comes next.
Some things will be
harder than
others. All of it will
hurt, especially the
joy, the love. Not
as it happens, but

at some future
point, when
things break,
when lives or
relationships are
lost, then the
weight of that
joy, that balloon
that lifted your
heart for a
moment or a
month or a
year or decades,
that weight will

turn to lead and settle on your
heart and it will hurt, but it will be
worth it, it was worth it, was it
worth it? Is the light turning? In the
infinite, there are always second
chances. If you're reading this, look
up. If you're reading this, there's still
time. If you're reading, if you're
breathing, if your heart is

ACKNOWLEDGMENTS

Thank you to the people of the Salton Sea and its nearby communities, the ones who hang on, the artists who pass through, the ones who get out and the ones who never can. What you've made out there is beautiful. Thanks as ever to my family—Aleks, Ollie, Mom, Dad, and Carl. I know long lists of names can be annoying, and I'm scared to start writing because I'll feel terrible for leaving people out, but I'm thankful to fellow writers and artists who've helped me believe in myself, whether giving me feedback, kind words, inviting me onto projects, or inspiring me with their works—Max Booth III, Lori Michelle, Kate Jonez, Eugene Johnson, Nikki Guerlain, Eric Miller, Xach Fromson, Kate Maruyama, Craig Wallwork, David James Keaton, Monica Drake, Derek Hynes, and Katarina Leigh Waters. You all make writing a less lonely place.

And thanks, of course, to Leonard Cohen. We're all still waiting for the miracle to come.

ABOUT THE AUTHOR

Michael Paul Gonzalez is the author of the novels *Angel Falls* and *Miss Massacre's Guide to Murder and Vengeance* and the short story collection *Carry Me Home: Stories of Horror and Heartbreak*. He wrote and produced the serial horror audio drama *Larkspur Underground*, available for free on iTunes and Stitcher. An active member of the Horror Writers Association, he resides in Los Angeles, a place full of wonders and monsters far stranger than any that live in the imagination. You can visit him online at MichaelPaulGonzalez.com

IF YOU ENJOYED BENEATH THE SALTON SEA,
DON'T MISS THESE OTHER TITLES FROM
PERPETUAL MOTION MACHINE . . .

LOST SIGNALS
BY MAX BOOTH III & LORI MICHELLE

ISBN: 978-1-943720-08-8

$16.95

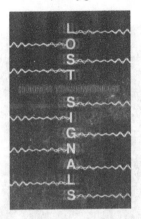

What's that sound? Do you feel it?

The signals are already inside you. You never even had a chance.

A tome of horror fiction featuring radio waves, numbers stations, rogue transmissions, and other unimaginable sounds you only wish were fiction. Forget about what's hiding in the shadows, and start worrying about what's hiding in the dead air.

With stories by Matthew M. Bartlett, T.E. Grau, Joseph Bouthiette Jr., Josh Malerman, David James Keaton, Tony Burgess, Michael Paul Gonzalez, George Cotronis, Betty Rocksteady, Christopher Slatsky, Amanda Hard, Gabino Iglesias, Dyer Wilk, Ashlee Scheuerman, Matt Andrew, H.F. Arnold, John C. Foster, Vince Darcangelo, Regina Solomond, Joshua Chaplinsky, Damien Angelica Walters, Paul Michael Anderson, and James Newman. Also includes an introduction from World Fantasy-award-winning author, Scott Nicolay.

WE NEED TO DO SOMETHING
BY MAX BOOTH III
ISBN: 978-1-943720-45-3
$12.95

A family on the verge of self-destruction finds themselves isolated in their bathroom during a tornado warning.

"Don't look now but Max Booth III is one of the best in horror, and he's only getting started." –Josh Malerman, author of BIRD BOX and MALORIE

Now a major motion picture!

ANTIOCH
BY JESSICA LEONARD
ISBN: 978-1-943720-49-1
$16.95

Antioch used to be a quiet small town where nothing bad ever happened. Now six women have been savagely murdered. The media dubs the killer "Vlad the Impaler" due to the gruesome crime scenes of his victims. Clues are drying up fast and the hunt for the monster responsible is hitting a dead end.

After picking up a late-night transmission on her short-wave radio, a local bookseller named Bess becomes convinced a seventh victim has already been abducted. Bess is used to spending her nights alone reading about Amelia Earhart conspiracy theories, and now a new mystery has fallen in her lap: one she might actually be able to solve.

Assuming she doesn't also wind up abducted.

The Perpetual Motion Machine Catalog

Antioch | Jessica Leonard | Novel

Baby Powder and Other Terrifying Substances | John C. Foster
Story Collection

Bone Saw | Patrick Lacey | Novel

Born in Blood Vols. 1 & 2 | George Daniel Lea | Story Collections

Crabtown, USA:Essays & Observations | Rafael Alvarez | Essays

Dead Men | John Foster | Novel

The Detained | Kristopher Triana | Novella

Eight Eyes that See You Die | W.P. Johnson | Story Collection

The Flying None | Cody Goodfellow | Novella

The Forest | Lisa Quigley | Novel

The Girl in the Video | Michael David Wilson | Novella

Gods on the Lam | Christopher David Rosales | Novel

The Green Kangaroos | Jessica McHugh | Novel

Invasion of the Weirdos | Andrew Hilbert | Novel

Jurassichrist | Michael Allen Rose | Novella

Last Dance in Phoenix | Kurt Reichenbaugh | Novel

Like Jagged Teeth | Betty Rocksteady | Novella

Live On No Evil | Jeremiah Israel | Novel

Lost Films | Various Authors | Anthology

Lost Signals | Various Authors | Anthology

Mojo Rising | Bob Pastorella | Novella

Night Roads | John Foster | Novel

The Nightly Disease | Max Booth III | Novel

Quizzleboon | John Oliver Hodges | Novel

The Ruin Season | Kristopher Triana | Novel

Patreon:
www.patreon.com/pmmpublishing

Website:
www.PerpetualPublishing.com

Facebook:
www.facebook.com/PerpetualPublishing

Twitter:
@PMMPublishing

Newsletter:
www.PMMPNews.com

Email Us:
Contact@PerpetualPublishing.com